WHAT DOES THE FUTURE hold in store? If you could, would you choose to ask?

There was a time once when the Three Fates sat in the corner of the young world and knitted like grandmothers for each newborn infant. They wove and worked and patterned each day of a man's life: from the first stitch to the last casting off.

And in those days, there were oracles, too, on the Earth—fortunetellers so sharp-eyed that they could see into the future, so heartless that they were prepared to say what they saw there. Would you have called on one? Would you have asked an oracle to tell your fortune?

What's the point of asking you? You wouldn't have been the one to decide. The Fates would have decided long in advance whether you made the journey or not. And what the Fates decided, no man could alter—not even Perseus. . . .

Also by Geraldine McCaughrean:

Casting the Gods Adrift
The Kite Rider
The Pirate's Son
The Stones Are Hatching
Stop the Train

⌘

Adaptations from the classics:

Moby Dick
El Cid
One Thousand and One Arabian Nights
Stories from Shakespeare

⌘

Titles in the Heroes Series:

Odysseus
Perseus
Theseus (Fall 2005)
Hercules (Fall 2005)

Perseus

RETOLD BY
Geraldine McCaughrean

Cricket Books/Chicago

HEROES

Library of Congress Cataloging-in-Publication Data

McCaughrean, Geraldine.
  Perseus / Geraldine McCaughrean.— 1st American ed.
     p. cm. — (Heroes)
  ISBN 0-8126-2735-0 (alk. paper)
  1. Perseus (Greek mythology)—Juvenile literature. I. Title. II. Series.

BL820.P5M33 2005
398.2′0938′02—dc22
                                                    2004020690

For Eli, Lucas, and Esau

Contents

The Monsters and Immortals
in PERSEUS

ATHENE—Goddess of War and Wisdom

ATLAS—a Titan who, as a punishment by Zeus, must hold up the sky forever

THE FATES—three Goddesses of Destiny who weave each person's future, creating an unchangeable fate

GORGONS—three hideous monsters with venomous serpents for hair

GRAEAE—three wise crones with one eye and one tooth among them; sisters of the Gorgons

HERA—Goddess of Marriage, wife of Zeus, and Queen of the Gods

HERMES—Messenger of the Gods

MEDUSA—the only mortal Gorgon of the three; turns men to stone

NYMPHS OF THE WEST—three beautiful sisters secluded on an unknown island; keepers of Pluto's Pack, the Helmet of Invisibility, and the Winged Sandals

ORACLE AT EPIDAURUS—the place where a serpentine fortuneteller reveals futures

PEGASUS—the white, winged horse born of the blood of Medusa; offspring of Medusa and Poseidon

PLUTO—God of the Underworld (also known as Hades)

POSEIDON—God of the Sea and Earthquakes

SEA MONSTER—terrifying monster created by Poseidon; terrorizes the city of Ammon and lusts for the blood of Princess Andromeda

ZEUS—Ruler of the Gods

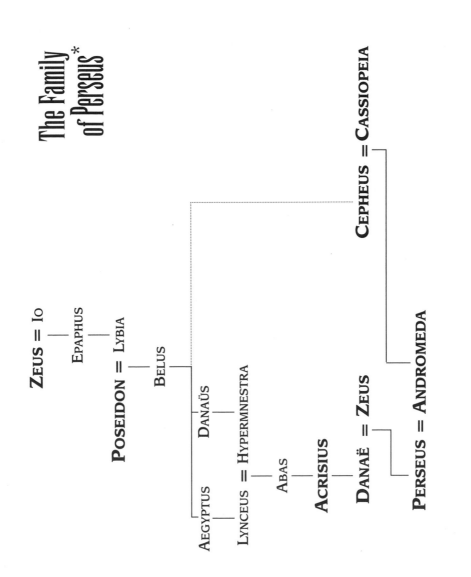

The Family of Perseus*

*This is only one version of Perseus's family tree.
Scholars are often in disagreement over the exact
lineages of the Immortals and humans of Greek
mythology.

Chapter One

For Fear of Things to Come

THEY HAVE NO feelings, you see. Oracles. How could they?

Suppose you could look into the future and read there every downfall, every disaster, every desire unfulfilled, every death and all decay, every dark damnation in store. Could you go on caring?

If oracles had feelings, they would hold back. They would bite their tongues. They would turn away their heads into the shadows and keep silent their secrets.

"There will be good times; there will be bad times," they could say. That much would be true. There is always good and bad to come.

But no. Their mouths let fall the future like water from a bubbling fountain, with never a thought for how it will poison those who eagerly drink it in. Still, poison is to be expected of snakes. And the oracle at Epidaurus was, after all, a serpent.

King Acrisius of Argos went to visit the Epidauran oracle to inquire whether he would ever have a son.

"You have a daughter. Your des-s-scendants-s will people a great nation. Be content," hissed the oracle.

King Acrisius hesitated. So many more questions crowded into his mind, so many things he wished to know about the future. Will my country's enemies attack? Will the rains come? Will the harvest ripen? Will my people thrive? He might have asked any of those. But no. He asked the one question that every foolish man wants to know: "How will I die . . . die . . . die?" The question echoed round the walls of the gloomy, comfortless temple.

"They all as-s-sk that," said the oracle, with a contemptuous flick of its green-scaled head. "How dull you are. How tedious-s-s." The yellow, lidless eyes rested on Acrisius as if he were already dead and forgotten. "Pers-s-seus-s-s," hissed the oracle.

"What's that? An illness? Is it painful? How? When?"

"Pers-s-seus-s-s," said the oracle again irritably. "Your grandson, Pers-s-seus-s-s, will kill you . . . in good time."

"But I haven't got a grandson!"

The oracle yawned. "You have a daughter, haven't you?"

"But she's not even—" Acrisius interrupted himself with a heartfelt cry that echoed round the temple. "When? When? When?"

"When your time is done," breathed the oracle, coiling itself like a rope on a ship's deck into a flat, tidy circle. "You have as-s-sked your fill. Come no more, Acris-s-sius-s."

The king stumbled on shaking legs out of the clammy temple and was stunned to his knees by the sunlight outside. Behind him, the oracle whispered to itself scornfully, "Why do they always-s as-s-sk it? They none of them think they will die. S-s-so why do they go on as-s-sking?"

"Danaë! My darling Danaë!" Acrisius said it a thousand times on his journey home. "My own daughter's son will kill me? Never! Such a gentle, loving girl! She would never allow it! Ah, she could never give birth to such an unnatural son!"

After another mile he thought, But suppose the child took after his father? What father? Danaë's not even married. And what monster could she marry who would breed such a son? No, no, the oracle is mistaken. Not possible. Not possible.

After another ten miles he thought, But suppose the child's a lunatic, moon-touched, or cursed with a dreadful temper, or clumsy, or given to accidents. . . . Poor Danaë. Better not to give life to such a brat . . . Better not to marry than to give life to such a brat . . . Better never to meet a man than to marry and give birth to such a brat . . . Better she were . . . Then Acrisius turned up his collar and looked round him, guilty at the thoughts in his own head.

• • •

On his return from Epidaurus, he set about building.

His architect said, "Yes, yes, I understand you. A high, round tower. But what is it for, Your Majesty?"

His clerk of works said, "Yes, yes, I will follow the plans—thick walls, no staircases, only one floor near the top. But what is it for, Your Majesty?"

His daughter, Danaë, said, "Yes, yes, Father. It's a remarkable piece of building. Very . . . er . . . tall. Very . . . interesting. People will come from far and wide to see it. But what exactly is it for?"

"Is it a watchtower?"

"Is it a lighthouse?"

"Is it a mill?"

"Is it a silo?"

"Is it a chimney?"

"And why does it have no door?"

Acrisius said not one word. When his tower was built, while the winches and hoists were still in place, he invited his daughter—his lovely, unmarried daughter, Danaë—to enjoy the view from the tower's summit. While he stood at the bottom, she rode in a brick basket up the funnel of stone to the wooden platform at the top.

"Oh, Father! I think the stonemason must sleep up here! There's a little bed. And a table. And a basket on a rope and . . ."

"And how is the view, Danaë, my dearest?" called the king. The echo made it sound like a sob in his throat.

4

Danaë crossed to the little, barred window. As she did so, there was a deafening clatter of scaffolding, and a squealing from the tackle block, and a snaking of falling rope. "Father! Father! The winch has gone! The hoist has collapsed! Help! How am I to get down? Oh, be quick, Father. It's a fearful height. I'm dizzy to look down! Father! Father?"

But though her calls tumbled down the tower like pebbles down a well—"Why, Father? Why?"—no one stood at the base to hear her.

"I'm sorry! I'm sorry! I'm so sorry!" murmured Acrisius, tripping on the folds of his robes as he ran toward the palace. His daughter's cries clamored out of the small, barred window like the peals of a bell at the head of a belltower. But he covered his head with his arms, his ears with his hands, and he howled down the noise: "She shan't have a son! She shan't marry and have a son! There'll be no grandson! There'll be no killing of grandfathers. Let her live there and die there. Well, and what's wrong with that?"

The eyes of his servants and ministers rested on him, empty of comment.

"Well? She can have anything she wants—food, games, dresses. . . . Well? She's only a woman, isn't she? She's mine to do with as I choose. And she'll never miss what she's never had!"

The eyes of his servants and ministers rested on him, but their mouths spoke not a word.

"Well? I could have killed her, couldn't I? I could have, couldn't I?"

The eyes of his ministers and servants rested on him with not so much as a raising of eyebrows.

"But someone tell her to be quiet!" he shrieked, driving his fingers into his ears until he coughed himself into a silence.

After a while, Danaë was silent, too. She stood long hours at the barred window of the tower and watched the sun rise, the moon set, the spring ripen, and the autumn leaves fall. She saw the dark shadow of the tower fall toward the palace like an accusing finger, and she saw her father cringing in the window of his chamber.

At first she called. And then she wept. And then she thought. And then she sang, for the sake of hearing a voice ring back off the curving walls.

The citizens of Argos looked up now and then and said, "She's singing again."

"I couldn't sing, could you?"

"She's a sweet girl."

"He's a cruel father."

"A stupid man . . ."

"A wicked king . . ." Then they shivered and went on their way.

But someone else heard Danaë singing and stopped to listen—stopped and listened and looked and liked what he heard and saw. High in heaven, Zeus, king of the gods, swung a leg lazily over the side of his hammock of cloud and peered down on the tower's round roof. Danaë stood warming herself in the beams of sun that slotted through the barred window and painted a bright, striped square on the floor.

As the sea has an endless appetite for the rivers of the world, so Almighty Zeus had an appetite for beautiful women. "Poor soul," he said mournfully. "So all alone," he said earnestly. "So badly treated," he said indignantly. "And so very pretty."

Standing in her pool of light, Danaë stretched herself and turned her face to the warmth of the sun. "Oh, for someone to talk to! Oh, for someone to share this loneliness! Did I ask so much of life that the Fates have abandoned me here? What would I ever ask for again if I only had my freedom? A little home somewhere—a husband to care for, maybe—a little baby . . ." Her arms cradled the air tenderly, and high above the tower a rumble of thunder sounded like a groan of longing.

Doesn't the largest river thread itself out of a tiny spring? Doesn't the largest bird hatch out of an egg? Can't all the words in the world be spoken by a single small mouth? It was no great feat, then, for Zeus, father of the gods, to thread his great form through the small, barred window of a prison tower. He simply transformed himself into a shower of gold and poured himself down a shaft of sunlight into Danaë's lonely cell.

Coins and ingots and gold dust pelted her like hail so

that she reeled and fell on her back and drew up her knees and cried out in fright. But it was not unpleasant—just a little startling.

When she got over her astonishment, Danaë gathered up the gold into her lap and sat turning it over in her fingers. It was warm to the touch, but then that is the nature of gold—warm and soft and pliable. It was not the first time Danaë had counted gold or fingered precious metals.

Though it was perhaps the first time the king of the gods had experienced anything so very agreeable.

After a time, when it was dark, she got up and went to the window. "You! Hey, you!" she called down softly to a passing soldier of the guard. "A skirtful of gold if you'll help me escape from this terrible prison!"

The guard slouched against the wall of the tower and snorted with laughter. "And where would you lay your hands on gold, Princess?"

Danaë lifted her lapful of treasure and tipped it out through the bars. Looking up, the astonished soldier saw a shimmering, glinting chute of spinning light cascading down on him. He threw up one arm across his face, to protect himself, and reached out the other hand, greedy for the gold.

But it was only a trick of the moonlight, for no coins or ingots of gold bombarded him. The spinning light seemed to dissolve away in midair, and the guard was sent sprawling by a sudden gust of wind.

So Danaë remained in her tower, alone. She might even have thought the shower of gold nothing but a dream but for an occasional flurry of gold dust round the floor when the winter wind blew in.

Nine months later, Danaë gave birth to a boy.

"A baby? She's had a baby? It's not possible!" cried King Acrisius when they told him. "She's been locked in that tower for two years! She hasn't so much as sneezed on a man! Don't bring me these lies!"

"A boy, Your Majesty," was all the messenger said. "She has called him Perseus."

"Kill it! Kill them both!" screamed the king, his voice breaking in the dryness of his throat. "Well? Why does nobody move? Why does nobody obey me?"

Ministers of government shuffled their feet. "It wouldn't be wise, Your Highness. The country would rise up against you. You . . . You've been less than popular since . . . since the . . . er . . . tower, Sire. We think there would be riots—open rebellion—protests—ballots—voting—republicanism."

Acrisius suppressed a cry of alarm. "Very well. Fetch a trunk."

"A trunk, Your Highness?"

"A trunk. A trunk. Are you deaf? A coffer—with a lid and a latch. Take it down to the beach . . . and break open the tower."

Then his ministers ran. They picked up the hems of

their robes and they ran—with crowbars and sledge and hammers and ropes and winches, and they broke open the walls of Danaë's tower. While they were doing so, the crying of her newborn baby rained down on them like the ringing from a belfry. So delighted were they at the king's change of heart that they hurried to fetch him just what he had asked for—a solid oak chest with a lid and a latch—and set it by the shoreline.

Only later in the day, as they watched it wallow out to sea, did they curse themselves for fetching it and spit on their own hands because they had helped Acrisius in his wickedness.

Chapter Two

An Unwelcome Suitor

FOR ACRISIUS HAD his soldiers force Danaë and her baby son into the wooden chest, closed the lid on them, and locked it with a key.

"Father! Father! What did I ever do that you should hate me so much?" cried the muffled voice of his daughter. "What crime did I commit that you should imprison me in the tower and now in this . . . this . . . coffin?"

But the only reply was the shriek of a sea gull and the slap of its big, orange feet as it strutted up and down the ridged lid of the floating trunk.

Back on the shore, hissed by the scornful sea, Acrisius hugged himself in both arms but would never again feel loved. His ministers looked at him with faces as hard as rocks, with eyes as blank as the seashore pebbles.

"Well? I didn't execute her, did I? I didn't kill the baby! Nobody can ever say I murdered them! I just . . . I just . . . sent them away." And the ministers' eyes turned away from the king and rested on the troughing ocean. Already the maze of waves hid the bobbing trunk from sight. Everyone there thought it had leaked already, already filled, already sunk with a silent thud to the crab-infested seabed and the shifting, corpse-cold dark.

A fresh wind was blowing. Skittering over the wave-tops, sharp as stones, a rattle of icy spray spattered Acrisius's face.

Watching from somewhere beyond the horizon, Zeus, king of the gods, was not well pleased to see his own son posted, like a message in a bottle, out to sea. He cut a notch in his lightning staff to remind him of a debt unpaid, a wrong unpunished, then swept home to the holy mountain of Olympus. The hem of his cloak sprinkled the ocean with hail behind him. The hail rattled (very like gold coins) on the lid of the wooden chest. And the slipstream swirling behind the great god dragged that portion of the sea, scarflike, into a different ocean where dolphins tugged it farther still in their beaks. Finally, the wooden chest grounded—*bang!*—on a shoal of whelky, submerged rocks. The brass bindings broke, the nails were jarred loose, the seams opened, and the sea rushed in.

If Dictys's nets had not at that very moment scooped up the remains of the wooden trunk into his little fishing boat, Princess Danaë would have surely become no more than a hank of hair and a rag of cloth washing to and fro in the water.

Dictys forced open the metal latch and lifted the lid.

To his astonishment, a pair of white arms reached out at once and placed into his slippery hands a baby boy.

"Warm him! Warm him, for the love of heaven!" cried Danaë, and she rose up out of the chest like the Goddess of Love first rose up from the waves.

Love herself could not have seemed more beautiful in Dictys's eyes. As he pushed the small, cold baby inside his shirt against the warmth of his chest, he found his heart beating fit to leap out through his gaping jacket.

"Your servant, Lady. Your eternal servant," was all he could say, all he could think. Danaë put her cold, wet hand into his, and stepped into the shelter of his boat.

And there, you might say, she stayed for eighteen years. And had they remained, the three of them, on that little fishing boat, the oracle's prophecies could never have come true.

But as soon as Danaë had told her story, Dictys was all impatience to present her to the king of his country. A princess—a great beauty—a mother and her son cast adrift on the sea and brought to the shores of his kingdom! It was surely news fitting for a king's ears. "And the palace is surely a far more fitting place for you to stay than my poor, little fisherman's hut," said Dictys breathlessly.

"I'm perfectly comfortable here," said Danaë, curled up in front of his hearth.

But nothing would prevent Dictys from rushing to the palace of King Polydectes with news of his wonderful discovery.

King Polydectes of Seriphus was a man of distinction. Not for him the scurrying, round-shouldered, guilty gait of Danaë's royal father. Polydectes walked with his chest thrown out and his cloak trailing, flicking his hands to right and left to draw attention to his many, many possessions. For Polydectes collected beautiful things—china, glassware, silver ornaments, gold plate, pictures, statues, chariots, trees, tapestries, lamps, clothes, furniture, armor, horses, and dancing girls.

Oh, and wives.

"You didn't gasp," said Polydectes, pursing his lips peevishly when Dictys was admitted to his presence. "Everyone always gasps at the amazing beauty of my palace."

Dictys bowed low and apologized. "I was so very breathless with running, Your Majesty. I've run all the way from the harbor!" And he told the king about Danaë and her baby cast out to sea in the wooden chest. But perhaps if Dictys had not been so quick to mention Danaë's beauty, then Polydectes might have simply yawned and gone back to watching his dancing girls.

"Did you say 'beautiful'?" asked the king, sliding languidly off his couch like a lizard. "How beautiful?"

"Oh, the angelfish with their streaming rainbow fins are not more beautiful, Your Majesty," said Dictys. He really did not mean to recommend Danaë like a carpet salesman selling a rug, and afterward he cursed himself for speaking so feelingly.

"I don't greatly care for fish," said Polydectes thoughtfully. "Except the stuffed variety. But you can tell this seagoing princess that once she's washed the seaweed out of her hair, she may come here to the palace. If she's as good as you say, I might condescend to marry her."

Then Dictys gasped, though not at the beauties of the king's royal palace. "What have I done?" he asked himself in horror.

Danaë had no wish to marry King Polydectes. She sent word to say so—politely, respectfully, and with due gratitude.

The king summoned her to the palace and, having once seen her, issued a royal proclamation that he would marry Princess Danaë the very next day.

"You do me a great honor, Your Majesty," said Danaë, "but I don't wish to marry you tomorrow."

"Next week, then. Not a day later," snapped the king.

"You misunderstand me, my lord. I mean that I don't wish to marry anyone at all."

When Danaë refused him a fourth and fifth time, the king became surly and cross. When she refused him for a year and then for ten years, it became an obsession with Polydectes. "I will have her. No woman refuses me!"

But Danaë chose to stay with Dictys the fisherman, and though they were poor and had nothing to eat but the fish Dictys caught, the three of them were happy: Danaë, Dictys, and Perseus.

15

Perseus grew like a pollarded willow—all the more beautiful for standing by the waterside and suffering the cuts of Fate. His hair leaped toward heaven in a thousand curled question marks, and his eyebrows seemed always raised in wonder. His eyes were so pale a brown that they were almost gold—round, like two golden coins. He learned a leaping confidence from the sea and a stillness from the rocks. He learned cunning from the wrasse that feels its way silently over the seabed and fierceness from the shark. He learned wisdom from the dolphin and recklessness from the bass who feeds under the pounding surf. But not even the whale calf, who swims in the great shadow of its mother through ice and storm, could teach Perseus anything about loyalty.

"I shall protect you, Mother!" he said every time King Polydectes sent his messenger to rattle at the door. "Though you have no husband to look after you, I shall take care of you and keep you from harm!"

He went fishing with Dictys, and as the tides counted in and counted out eighteen years, Perseus grew to be a man.

"I've done asking! I've done requesting! I've done inviting!" raged King Polydectes. "Send troops to the fisherman's hut. Send them when the fisherman's away at sea! Tell them to fetch the woman Danaë here. I will have her! I must have her for my wife!" The idea of Danaë was by now a madness in his blood. All his other fine possessions held no delight for him. All his other wives seemed ugly. He only wanted what he could not have. The wanting nagged and chewed and clawed at him. "I will marry the wretched Princess Danaë, and I'll marry her today!"

So the soldiers beat at the door of the fisherman's hut. "Open up! Open up, in the name of the king!"

The door opened, and there stood a young man—hardly more than a boy—with a startling shock of golden hair and pale, round, almost golden eyes. "Good day, gentlemen," he said brightly.

"We've come for the woman, Danaë." The captain of the guard stepped forward, but Perseus put up one hand.

"You are welcome, I say, to stand on our doorstep. But come one step inside, and I'll be obliged to throw you out."

Meanwhile, at the palace, King Polydectes put on his finest robe and turned down the covers of his great marriage bed. "I should have done this long before now!" he shouted at the parrot dozing on the perch by the window. "I'll teach this woman how very unwise it is to slight a king—very unwise!"

"King very unwise," repeated the parrot.

Eagerly, Polydectes watched from the chamber window for the patrol to bring his bride. At last they straggled into view—a scuffle here, a flurry of dust there, a raising of voices, a few smudged words. Polydectes was excited to think of Danaë struggling like a pretty moth in a web.

17

But strain his eyes as he might, he could not see her among his soldiers; he could only see them squabbling and brawling among themselves.

" . . . head hurts . . ."

" . . . took us by surprise . . ."

" . . . got the better of you, you mean . . ."

" . . . who's going to tell the king . . . ?"

"Tell me what?" bawled Polydectes from the window. "Where's my bride? Where's Danaë?"

"It was that son of hers, Your Majesty! He took us by surprise! He's a little demon, Your Majesty . . . strong beyond his years . . . used magic, I'd say." They poured out their excuses at the king's feet, then delivered the message Perseus had sent them away with: "Say my mother shall marry whom and when she pleases!"

Polydectes wiped the flecks of foam from his lips and slammed the shutter closed. "Perseus! I'll wager it's that lad who's poisoned his mother against me! Well, if he's the only obstacle . . . Wisht! Tread carefully, Polydectes. You can't kill the brat and hope his mother will love you after," Polydectes said to himself as a sneering smile broke over his face. "No. This calls for subtlety—a plan, a plot. If Perseus is the problem, Perseus must be put out of the way."

So the king looked round among the little tribal kingdoms and found himself a princess—any sorry little princess—and announced that he would marry her.

Silver trumpets swore to it, and proclamations spoke it from every pillar and tree: "Rejoice and pay tribute! King Polydectes will marry the Princess Nemo! Presents will be graciously received." And he let it be known that his heart had sickened of the obstinate Princess Danaë.

It was a great relief. Danaë unclenched her anxious little fists, and the fisherman Dictys laid aside his rusty, old sword (for he had thought to fight to the death rather than see Danaë forced into marriage). "I shall catch fish enough to feed the wedding guests," he said. "That will be my tribute to the king."

"My gratitude and blessing will be my tribute," said Danaë, who had not a penny to call her own.

"And I shall pay tribute, too!" Perseus declared recklessly.

Standing close by, according to the king's instructions, was a palace courtier. He immediately burst out laughing—a loud, forced, humorless laugh that drew every eye. "Did you hear that? Perseus is going to pay tribute! Little Perseus is going to give the king a wedding present! Barefoot Perseus! One-shirt Perseus! Fish-stinking Perseus is going to offer tribute to the king! What will it be, then? A few seashells? Or a piece of driftwood?"

The color rose into Perseus's cheeks as it rises into the sky at sunset. His eyes flashed brighter than freshly minted gold. And he ran all the way to the palace and knelt on one knee in front of King Polydectes. Strangely enough, the king seemed to be expecting him.

"I hear you mean to bring tribute to me and my new bride, lad. How very kind. The duke here has promised ten horses. The count over there is giving a summer house. And what had you in mind to give me?"

"Name it, Your Majesty! Name it, and I shall bring it! You shall have whatever you ask, Sire!"

So Perseus fell into the king's trap, and the king laughed and snorted into his cup of wine and spattered his clothes blood-red. *"Anything,* Perseus? Well, let's make it . . . no, no. Let me see . . . I wouldn't like to insult you with a paltry challenge. . . ."* He strolled up and down the room, pretending to rack his brains. "Let's make it the . . . no, no, that would be too difficult, surely. . . . Although you did say anything, didn't you?"

"Anything, Your Majesty!"

"Then let's make it the head of Medusa!" The king turned quickly so as to catch the tremor of fear and horror that must surely shake Perseus to the core. But he was disappointed. Perseus did not so much as flinch.

"Very good, Your Majesty. The head of Medusa. It will be my honor to lay Medusa's head at your feet, Sire, before the next moon has waned!"

Braggarty little fool, thought the king, smirking as best he knew how. That's the last boast he'll make.

At the door, Perseus turned and seemed about to ask for something. Mercy? Pity, perhaps? The king's eyebrows lifted superciliously. "Yes? Was there something, boy?"

Perseus blushed, shook his head, and left. But in the courtyard outside, he stopped a palace servant and asked in a little whisper, "Excuse me troubling you. But do you happen to know what or who Medusa is?"

Chapter Three

Taking Up Arms

MEDUSA WAS A thing of sea chanteys and travelers' tales and nightmares. Medusa was Fear itself, clumsily parceled up so that she spilled out into rumor and legend. She was a hissing at the corner of the world, a horror just out of sight of the corner of the eye. Medusa was vile.

She had been beautiful once—beautiful such that the eye that saw her could not bear to look away. Her eyes had been so beautiful that the Sea-Shaker, the Earthquake-Maker, the sea god himself, Poseidon, loved her and wanted to possess her. But she was a flirt and a tease and put Poseidon to the indignity of chasing her all over the city of Athens. The waves of the ocean-god sluiced through the streets—a tidal wave of desperate passion.

Medusa ran at last into the purified and holy temple of the goddess Athene, and there she allowed her chaser to catch her. The building was over-arched by surging water, which swept into the temple and tumbled the beautiful Medusa in a glittering embrace.

But oh, when he withdrew, Poseidon's wave left the sacred holy altar stained white and the walls caked with salt and the offerings of the worshipers scattered about and ruined. So angry was the goddess Athene when she saw this vandalism and saw how Poseidon and Medusa had defiled her holy place on the Earth, that she cursed Medusa and made her as ugly as her two immortal sisters, Euryale and Stheno. Poseidon looked at her once and banished her and her sisters to the driest desert in the world—to Libya—so that he might never lay eyes on her again. And Medusa swore, there and then, that whosoever she laid eyes upon . . .

"But how is she vile?" Perseus asked the fisherman Dictys.

"No one has lived to say."

"Then if you can't tell me what she is or why she's hideous, won't you tell me where I can find her?"

"No. I don't know. And if I did, boy, I would tear out my tongue rather than tell you. You're the light of your mother's eye, and if you go on this foolish quest, you will leave her all in darkness." And he pulled his cloak over his face and would not speak another word about Medusa. But Perseus was as determined as ever to carry out his promise to the king.

From the terraces of Olympus, Medusa was just a small, distant, green, squirming thing. A whole forest of cedar trees had been planted to block the view a little so that the gods and goddesses should not be put off their breakfasts.

"I have a thing or two to do down there," said Zeus, greatest of the gods, waving a hand toward the distant landscape.

His wife, Hera, lifted her brown eyes, lash-fringed like the deep carpets of the silent Underworld. "What kind of a thing, husband?"

"Oh—dreams to deliver to young heroes," said Zeus generally. "That sort of thing."

"Which particular young hero?" asked Hera, trying to follow the line of his eye when, every few moments, he darted a glance toward the shores of Seriphus.

Zeus tugged at his beard irritably. His wife was disagreeably shrewd and took it to heart whenever she found out about his little love affairs. Most unreasonable. What were a few paltry kisses? And couldn't he spend his kisses where he chose? His mouth fell into a pout. What were a few extra sons scattered about the Earth, strong as bulls, with the valor of lions or with eyes like golden coins. And Zeus could not help being interested in them, could he? His human sons?

After a day or so, the king of the gods got up and tiptoed away, hoping nobody would notice. Weather fronts closed behind him, the blue stratosphere buckled, and the holy mountain shook so that berries fell from the bushes and streams changed course. But the gods, sprawled idly along the terraces, pretended not to notice the ruler of heaven picking his way down toward the plain. Only Hera breathed fast and furious through her regal nose and said, "Bastards!" Her nymphs-in-waiting pretended not to hear.

Perseus, lying on his face in bed, had thought he was fully awake, puzzling over how to find Medusa. But a sudden milkiness clouded his thoughts. He lay spread-eagled between waking and sleeping, dimly conscious of being unable to turn over.

Zeus leaned low over his son and whispered in his ear: "Go to the ghastly, gray-eyed Graeae. Ask what they would rather not tell you. Ask where you may find the Nymphs of the West. You hear? But take care, boy. Take care."

All the doors and windows in the house banged, and Perseus rolled over onto his back, suddenly wide awake. "I had the strangest dream. . . ." he started to say. But Dictys had already risen and gone out fishing, and his mother, troubled by dreams of her own, was scurrying about, fastening the shutters and bolting the doors.

By the time Zeus returned to Olympus, he trailed behind him a dismal train of anxiety that bent trees at the shoulder and creased the clouds into a scowl. He gnawed his lip and threw himself down on his throne with his fists knotted in his beard. The lesser gods pulled their robes closer round them against the chilling of the air.

"A fine young man, that," said Hermes loudly to Athene, casually preening the feathers on his heels.

"A fine warrior lad, yes," said Athene, examining the point of her spear.

"Who is? What?" Zeus looked up.

"Oh, we were just discussing that boy Perseus, son of Danaë. An excellent little hero in the making. Remarkable background. Nobody quite knows who his father was—someone quite exceptional, that's plain."

Zeus sat back on his throne and stroked the knots out of his beard. "Now that you speak of him, I think I do recall the boy. Good family, you think?"

"Oh, undoubtedly. And so handsome, too."

A glint of pleasure crept into Zeus's eye like a single fish into a lake. "Now that you mention it, I do believe I've seen him once or twice. Didn't I hear somewhere that he's made some wild, foolish promise to find Medusa and cut off her head? Yes, I'm sure I did."

"How very brave!" "How enterprising!" said Hermes and Athene simultaneously.

Zeus looked pleased and only a little suspicious.

"In that case, I shall lend him my sickle sword!" declared Hermes.

"And I shall lend him my shield!" cried Athene.

Zeus beamed with delight. "How nice! How very generous! It pleases me greatly to see you taking such an interest in the little people of the Earth. Encouraging enterprise. Helping the courageous. Yes, indeed.

Excellent!" He jumped up from his throne and went to deal with affairs of the Divine State, a new spring in his ten-league stride.

Hermes and Athene looked at each other, and the goddess of war shrugged. "Well, I can't bear it when he sulks. Besides . . . I'd be glad to see Medusa's head in a bag."

"Why?" asked Hermes, startled by her ferocity.

"I hate her. Never mind why," said Athene, who did not like to speak of that white salt caking the walls and altar of her holy temple. "I hate her, that's all. So let's help that bastard Perseus as much as we're able."

They spat on their palms and shook hands in a pact: no word of helping Zeus's son must ever reach Hera, his jealous wife.

At each temple in turn, Perseus prayed for the help of the gods on his quest to find and kill Medusa. As he turned away from the altar of the goddess of war, a dazzle of light struck him in the face like a blow. An oval metal shield lay on the steps. Perseus thought it must have been left lying in the hot sun and had grown incandescent, for it was so bright that it left scorch marks on his vision. But when he picked it up, it weighed no more than a mirage—a shiny, eye-deceiving pool of light. He half expected it to disappear off his arm.

Realizing that here was a gift from the gods, he shut his eyes tight in thankful prayer. Behind him, there was the sound of a scythe striking down a shock of corn, then a metallic twanging. He spun round and saw a sword—a curved sickle of a sword—wedged deep in the solid stone of the temple step, its hilt pointing the way he should go.

Perseus turned his golden eyes to the sky and thanked whatever power had sent him these strange, fantastical presents. He took up the sword and set off running, thinking not to stop till he found the Graeae (whatever they were) and Medusa (whatever she was) and sliced off her head. "How can I fail with the gods helping me!" he crowed.

His steps led him directly to the seashore, where the sand made him sink and stagger, and the sea barred his way. His fingers accidentally brushed the sharp blade of the sickle sword, and drops of blood spotted the stainless face of the silver shield.

Then the breaking waves seemed to say, "You are still mortal, Perseus—a thing of flesh and blood—a weak, vain thing that will one day die." And his heart quailed inside him as he stood beside the vast ocean, on the shore of an unfriendly world.

Far away, in a kingdom Perseus knew nothing about, blood also spattered the seashore. And bones littered the sand. And deep footprints filled up with water on the rising tide. They were not human footprints, but hooked, lizardly tracks scuffed through by the great following

scar of a dragging tail. And the bones and blood were not human bones and blood, but all that was left of goats and sheep and pigs tethered among the dunes. So far, the people of Ammon had fed the sea monster on livestock. So far, they had kept it away from the bolted city gates with tethered sacrifices.

It was not enough. Each time the monster erupted from the sea like a tongue from a mouth, it devoured their offerings quicker than the time before. Then, shuffling on toward the city wall, it dangled its dewlapped head over the palisades and let its saliva drip. They could hear it panting, they could hear it grind its teeth, they could hear the hooked feet scratch at the wall. One day soon it would shoulder its way through the crumbling masonry and take the meal it craved—human flesh.

Chapter Four

The Gray-Eyed Graeae

LIKE A WIRE pulled tight, the western horizon thrums and trembles for one fraction of a blue second as the sun sets. The sound of it echoes through the whole hollow ocean. And in this region of shadow, where the floating islands of the world have drifted and collided and grown together like cartilage, live the Graeae.

Death never sails this far, so they never die. Only their bodies die, little by little, round them. A hand withers. A shoulder droops. A spine closes, vertebra by vertebra, into a brittle, rigid stick. So long have they stayed there, decayed there, that only one eye remains among the three, and only one has a tooth in her jaw.

But such an eye! It can see a voyager coming a hundred miles away. And such a tooth! It can eat him at a sitting and leave nothing for the gulls.

"Give me the eye, sister! It is my turn for the eye!" The seeing Graea claws the eye from its socket with a big-jointed finger and fumbles it into the outstretched palm of her sister. For they share the eye, all three.

"Give me the tooth, sister. I have a sailor here ripe for the eating!" The chewing Graea claws the tooth out of her black gums and fumbles it into the outstretched palm of her sister. For they share the tooth, all three.

Only while the eye was out did Perseus dare to move or blink or breathe. Only in that moment of blindness did he dare to crawl closer across the Graeae's midden of litter.

"What's that, Sister One? I thought I heard a rattle of bones. Is someone near? Give me the eye, quickly!"

"I look and I see nothing, Sister Two. It is not your turn yet for the eye."

"My mouth is watering, Sister. I could swear someone eatable was near. Give me the eye!"

"I look and I see no one, Sister Three. Wait your turn, can't you? Wait your turn."

Only as the eye changed hands did Perseus creep closer and closer to the foul sisters squatting on their haunches round a cauldron of boiling jellyfish and sea slugs.

"Give me the eye, Sister. It is my turn for the eye!"

So, like an oyster gouged from its shell, the single, soft, wet, gray eye is scooped out of its socket. "Here, then. Don't snatch, Sister! You might damage it!"

"Who snatched? Who snatched? It was my turn, and you've given the eye to Sister Three! Sister Three! Give it to me and wait your turn, you selfish hag!"

"Who, me? I don't have it. I didn't take it! Have you dropped it, you clumsy crone? Have you dropped our eye in the dirt? You fool!"

"I didn't drop it! I haven't touched it!"

"Well, a hand took it from my hand! One of you took it! Admit! Admit!"

"I admit," said Perseus. "I . . . have the eye."

The voice was so close to their ears that they swatted and snatched at it as they would a mosquito. Their purse-gathered lips opened in gasps of surprise and howls of rage. He lifted one plait of brittle gray Graea hair and rested it in the palm of another Graea.

"Sister! I have it by the hair! Give me the tooth so I can bite the thief to pieces!"

"Sister! Sisters! It has me by the hair! Give me the tooth so I can bite off its head!"

But out of the tangle of knotty hands, Perseus plucked the tooth as well, then sprang away to a safer distance. Six old hands patted and scraped the dirty ground, searching, hunting, desperate.

"Peace, sisters, and let me help you. Have you lost something? Let me help you find it, with my two good eyes."

The Graeae crawled toward him across the ground, reaching and snatching toward the sound of his voice. He skipped out of reach. "It has our tooth! It has our eye! Oh, sisters! What shall we do!"

Perseus said, "What can you mean? Can it be this

32

you're looking for? This sharp yellow tooth like the head of an ax, and this one soft, wet, gray, slippery eye? Surely not. Such ugly things. I think I'll throw them into the sea."

"No, no!" The Graeae froze, heads up, hands outstretched.

"Or shall I tread them underfoot?"

"No, no!" The Graeae scurried closer, their tears only in their voices, for they had no eyes for crying.

"So shall I sell them to you for a word or two of wisdom?"

"Give us back our eye! Give us back our tooth!"

"Or shall you starve in everlasting darkness?"

"WHAT DO YOU WANT?" they howled.

"Tell me where I may find the Nymphs of the West," said Perseus. "I need their help to find and kill the Gorgon called Medusa."

The Graeae, supported on knuckles and knees, sagged pitifully. "The Nymphs of the West? That secret is all we have left of value!" said Sister One. "While we keep the sight of them hidden from all human eyes, no one can compare our old age with their youth! We shall keep the secret of them until they are grown old like us. Then you may know."

"Then I shall toss this eye and this tooth into the cauldron with the jellyfish and the sea slugs," said Perseus briskly, and indeed he almost dropped the slippery eye, because his hand was wet with sweat.

"NO! Give us back our precious parts, and we will tell you!"

"Tell me, and I'll give you back your parts. Speak!"

The Graeae sank down, like torn sacks emptying. They slumped along the ground. "Follow the weed line. Follow it to their cave on the other side of the kingdom," said Sister Two.

"You fool, Sister! Now he'll never give us back our parts!"

Perseus was indignant. "What do you take me for, ladies? Here! Here's your precious eye, and here's your tooth. I, Perseus, honor my bargains!" (But even so, he threw their stolen parts onto the ground among the three. And when he last looked back, they were in danger of kneeling or leaning or slapping a hand down on the cold, wet, slippery, round, gray eye.

"Wait till I have it!" shrieked one. "Listen how I'll tear him like bread in the breaking!"

"Calmly, Sister! Calmly!" said another, squatting back on her haunches as she pushed home the single, dirty tooth. "If that thief out there thinks he's going to kill Medusa, he'll be turned to rock like the rest soon enough. Rock, heart and brain. Rock, lights and liver. Rock. Rock. Rock!" And she rolled on the balls of her ancient feet and laughed, for want of an eye to weep.

He followed the line of seaweed that circled the shore of that blue-black land. Whether the weed floated on the third wave or drew a flyblown line along the high-water mark, he followed it. And it led him to the mouth of a cave. He had leaned one hand against the entrance, to untangle the seaweed from round his feet, when a single vowel echoed down the cave.

"O-o-oh!"

He looked up and saw a girl as young as the Graeae were old, as beautiful as they were ugly, as naked as they were ragged, and as happy as they were sad.

"Oh, sisters!" she exclaimed softly after a moment spent staring at Perseus. "This is nice. Do come and see this."

Her two sisters came printless over the wet, sandy floor of their cave. "Is it a stork?" they said. "It's standing on one leg."

"Did it come out of the sea or out of the air? It is nice, yes, Sister. Such pretty eyes."

"I'm looking for the Nymphs of the West," said Perseus, and the girls scattered, as angelfish scatter at the blundering in of a shark. Curiosity soon brought them back.

"Did it speak?" said one.

"It looks rather like us, in a two-legged sort of way." She dropped her voice to a whisper. "Do you suppose it's one of the gods?"

"I'm not one of the gods," said Perseus. "I'm just a person—" He was about to say "the same as you," but looking them up and down there, this was blatantly untrue. "I'm just a man."

"What's a man?" said the Nymphs, who had lived unseen, unknown, unvisited all their lonely, lovely lives. "Is that like a sailor? We've heard tell of sailors."

So Perseus tried to explain. And when he had told them about men, he told them about cities and ships, clothes and chariots, horses and sheep, maize and apples, money and markets, kings and beggars, wars and festivals. It was all new and strange to them; they had heard none of it before. He tried to tell them about Love, too, but found he knew nothing about it and fell silent.

The Nymphs sprang and skipped about him while he talked, stroking his hair and plucking at things. "You're wonderful! You're making it all up! You're amazing! Take us with you and show us these things!"

Perseus apologized and said he regretted that he could not, at least until his work was done. "But you can teach me now, and tell me what I don't know. Where can I find Medusa, and how can I kill her?"

The Nymphs looked suddenly sad. They would not answer at first. One of them, twirling her fingers in Perseus's hair remarked, "It must be awful to be a rock." Frankly, Perseus thought it rather an irrelevant comment.

Then they drew him by the hand into their cave and showed him a painting on the wall. The oldest Nymph pointed in turn to three ghastly, winged women, saying: "Stheno . . . Euryale . . . Medusa."

A coldness gripped at Perseus's skeleton, and he found it difficult to move; the portraits were so vile that his gorge heaved. The three faces staring out from the wall were round, with flat, splayed noses and tongues dangling from between tusklike teeth. They were crudely drawn, he told himself, for the hair was a daub of fat green strands, not hanging down but standing out in all directions. He looked more closely, and his flesh sweated drops as cold as those that ran down the cave walls. They were not locks of hair sprouting from the heads at all.

They were snakes.

"Medusa turns things into rocks," said the oldest of the Nymphs. "Anything that looks at her."

"How do you know?" asked Perseus. "You've never left this beach, this cave. You've never met anybody but each other!"

The Nymphs shrugged and sucked their thumbs and scuffed the sand with their toes. "We just know. We've always known. I suppose we were born knowing. We were put here to know, I suppose—by the gods. We have the Things-to-Keep-Safe, after all."

"What are they?"

The Nymphs sniggered at his ignorance. "The Things, of course. For the One-Who-Will-Come. The Helmet and the Pack and the Shoes." They had gone back to examining him, unfastening and refastening his belt and unpicking the seams of his tunic and licking the intriguing drops of sweat off his neck.

"Do you suppose that could be me?" asked Perseus modestly.

The idea quite overwhelmed them. They rushed about the beach bumping into each other and tugging at their hair. They shrieked and laughed and wept and yelped, "Him! It's him! He's the One-Who-Will-Come! He is! He is! We knew it all along!"

They fetched from the cave a black, bulging shoulder bag and laid it at his feet with all the pride of cats presenting a dead bird or a half-eaten mouse. The bag was so black that it seemed to absorb all the light: he could not see what weave of cloth it was, but it smelled slightly dank and moldy. "The Pack of Pluto," said the Nymphs.

"Pluto, the god of the Underworld?"

But they only shrugged. That was the name they had always known, always used.

Perseus pushed his hand into the bag and snatched it out again. He had touched something warm and fluttering like a bird. He tipped the bag upside down on to the beach, and a helmet and a pair of sandals fell out. The sandals had feathers decorating their heels—rather unmanly and tasteless, thought Perseus, who preferred plain clothes himself. But as they lay on the beach, the feathery shoes began to tremble. They rolled onto their soles and pattered shyly round Perseus and roosted again alongside his feet. The Nymphs were enchanted. Perseus felt a little foolish, but he put on the sandals anyway.

And the next thing he knew, he was walking off the ground. He found footholds in the air and sprinted up among the sea gulls. "I can fly!"

It was hard, at first, to keep his head from tumbling between his feet and not to turn upside down like the clapper in a bell. But before long he stood in the air like a swimmer treading water in an ocean of sunlight.

He shouted out his thanks to the gods and settled gently onto the beach. The Nymphs were nowhere to be seen. Wedging his shining shield into the sand to serve as a mirror, he picked up the helmet that had also been in the bag, put it on, and stood back to admire himself.

Nothing.

The shield's perfect mirror showed him each blade of grass, each dune, each sandpiper, each dying wave. But no Perseus. The Nymphs, who had fled from the wonder of his flying, crept back out of their cave. "Ah. He's gone. The-One-Who-Comes has flown away and left us with nothing but his shield. . . ."

"O you gods!" cried Perseus in horror. "Is this a punishment for my boasting? Have you taken my body away from me? Have you turned me into sand? Am I a spirit? Am I dead? Is that all my sandals were for—to fly me to the Underworld?" His voice echoed deep inside the cave, but there was no reply. He kicked at the sand, and it hissed against the bright shield. He ripped off the helmet and threw it down in disgust.

And there he stood, his fear and fury reflected in the shield's mirror, and there lay Pluto's Helmet of Invisibility spinning on its bright, miraculous crest, jaw straps flying.

"Nymphs! Nymphs! Where are you? Come out and speak to me! Come back and tell me where to find the Medusa! I can fly! I can make myself invisible! What monster is safe from me? I could kill the whole world and never stop for breath!" And he swung his curved sword and laughed out loud. "What can Medusa do to me, the darling of the gods?!"

"Kill you, what else?" said the oldest Nymph from where she stood in the mouth of the cave. "She has only to sit where she sits, and you have only to look at her to be turned into stone. How will you kill her without look-ing at her?"

She was so certain he would die that Perseus faltered, and the showy flourish of his borrowed sword went astray and caught the rock of the cavern entrance. The impact jarred his arm in its socket and bruised his hand. He dropped the sword and put out his fingers to touch the damp stone. The words of the Nymphs rang round his head: "It must be awful to be a rock."

Far away in the kingdom that so far troubled Perseus not at all, the boastful King Cepheus bragged that his city walls could keep out any sea monster. But the people did not believe him. Neither did they believe that the sea monster would be fended off forever with goats, sheep, and cattle. Besides, their livestock was gone. They were living on bread. In fact, they were starving for lack of bread.

And every night the sea monster came and hung its head over the city walls and drooled its saliva onto the streets.

Chapter Five

The Gorgons

IT WAS LIKE watching a shrimp stray into the fronds of an anemone or a fly bumble into a spider's web. For the gods, watching from the heights of Olympus, it was sport to see unwary travelers meet the Gorgons.

How did the travelers come there? Sometimes sandstorms sent them astray in the heart of the desert. Or sometimes it was the misreading of a map. For some, a reckless dare. Or a stampeding camel, carrying its rider off the desert trail. Or the rumor of a magic place. For a dozen reasons, travelers regularly came to that barren everlastingness of yellow sand where the horizon vibrates like hot wire. But they never came away.

At the center of the desert stood the three Gorgons. The great desert winds had long since torn away their shadows and carried them round the world to drop as nightmares on the pillows of a thousand beds.

But even the worst nightmares could not compare with the sight of the Gorgons: those bony, stumpy wings, those snouting noses, those tusks bulging through rubbery lips, those dangling tongues, those eyes oozing red rheum, those serpents writhing out of skulls to knot and flicker in scaly green tresses. The Gorgons' eyelids drooped idly, for their snaky hair had a thousand eyes to scan the desert for passersby. Stheno, Euryale, and Medusa crouched in a seeming forest of stalagmites— rocky pillars rounded and shaped by the wind, caked in desert salt and stained by the droppings of vultures.

Look close. Those are not stalagmites. Those stumps are all that remain of travelers who died where they stood, in the single split second of seeing Medusa.

Imagine feeling your flesh creep with horror, the tiny hairs stand up rigid on your forearms, and looking down in time to see those hairs turn brittle, that hand turn gray and lose its pattern of blue veins. Imagine your sleeve suddenly weighing like stone, your flesh like bone, your feet becoming sealed to the rocky ground; your joints freeze, your muscles stiffen, the blood stops still, the heart falls like a boulder through the hollow of your body, the brain drops into the jawbone, the eyeballs dry and harden into blind, round pebbles. Then stillness, darkness, nothing . . . forevermore.

That was how death came to the travelers who strayed into the lair of the Gorgons. That was what the gods regularly watched—unmoved—from the heights of Olympus, like watching a shrimp sucked into an anemone or a fly bumbling into a spider's web.

Only when Perseus, son of Almighty Zeus, was flying

in his winged sandals toward the Gorgons' desert did the gods stir themselves uneasily and muster along the parapets of heaven and whisper to one another, peep and peer earthward, and twist their gauzy robes between anxious fingers. The rumor had quickly spread—that Perseus's fate was of particular interest to Zeus.

"Such a pleasant boy," said Athene. "Those golden eyes. Most appealing."

"So very reckless."

"So very daring."

"So very pious."

"So very promising."

"Oh yes. I'll find a good place for him in the Halls of the Dead." They all turned and stared at Pluto. "Well? You don't fool yourselves, do you, that he can succeed? How is he to kill Medusa without looking at her? Feel his way? Blunder into her with his eyes shut? Grope up her backbone and take hold of a handful of hair and one, two, off-with-her-head? Suppose he picks the wrong one? Stheno and Euryale are immortal. He may be invisible with my old helmet on, but then what? So he'll be an invisible rock instead of a visible one. So the vultures will fly into him and break their beaks, and the Gorgons will stub their toes against him. No, I'm telling you, by sunset I'll have to go down there and chisel his soul out of his body and take it inside my helmet down to the Underworld. That's the only compliment I'll pay to your Perseus there. He can't hope for better."

The gloomy god of the Underworld was startled by a sudden tightening in his black robe, as Zeus took hold of him from behind by collar and sash and shook him furiously. "Silence! Unless you want me to pitch you down to your everlasting halls and bolt the doors to keep you there. Where is Hermes? He must carry a message for me to the Gorgons and forbid them, in my name, to harm any more mortals!"

But the Gorgons were creatures of the Earth and loathed the gods for their beauty and had sworn never to obey the commands of Zeus the Almighty.

"Where's Athene? She must go to the boy and tell him it's impossible! It can't be done. Perseus must give up his attempt. Let him put some other head into his pack. I'll give him some monster's muzzle to take to Polydectes instead!"

The gods and goddesses turned away their heads, embarrassed to see their king howl and rage with fear. Zeus raised his fist, and in it was a thunderbolt large enough to break the horizon's trembling wire and shatter the Gorgons and their forest of rocks.

Then his wife, Hera, came and stood on the parapet of heaven between Zeus and his target. "Husband! You disturb all Olympus with your noise! What great disaster is about to happen that can make the king of heaven lose his dignity? Is a god in danger? Is one of the Immortals in peril? No? Then why such a shameful display? For a little mortal? A speck of flesh? A comma in history? Anyone would think this boy meant something special to you. One foolish little worshiper? Since when did we reach down and dabble in Fate? Even the noble hero Odysseus never stirred you to this kind of passion. Tell me, husband. Why should you concern yourself with this Perseus?"

Then Zeus might have said, "Perseus is my son. What's that to you? I am king of the gods. I'll father what children I like. I'll do as I please."

But then there would have been a rift in heaven—civil war like sheet lightning in the skies, and chaos. All these thoughts passed through Zeus's mind as he stared into the liquid brown eyes of his wife. And he did not say, "Perseus is my son." He said: "You are right, my dear. What is the fate of one young mortal? It's just that this boy—what's his name again?—Perseus, showed uncommon promise. And you know how sentimental I am. Pah! Let him go! What's it to me?" Then he pulled the hood of his robe forward over his head and walked away across the sky, stepping from cloud to cloud.

The gathering of gods broke up, with awkward gestures and muttered comments, and left none but Hera looking down from the parapets of heaven. An unpleasant sneer buckled her top lip. "Now, Perseus—look on the Gorgons and be turned to stone, and let the sands blast you and the vultures perch on you and the winds grind you down to dust!"

Sunlight flared up off the shield Perseus was carrying

across his back as he flew; it reflected so brightly that the stab of it hurt Hera's eyes, and she had to look away.

Perseus knew better than anyone how difficult it would be to cut off Medusa's head without looking at her. He considered waiting until the moon had set and following the sound of the hissing snakes. But how then could he be certain of beheading the right Gorgon? Besides, the night is rarely so black as to hide a thousand pairs of watching eyes or the black bulk of a body against the paler sand. How much of a glimpse must he catch of Medusa to be turned to stone? He had no way of knowing. Like a child peeping out between its fingers, he had a great yearning to see what could be so very terrible that it turned a man to stone.

Perseus knew when he was approaching the lair of the Gorgons. Even the birds were not immune to the dreadful magic of Medusa's eyes. Those that looked down as they flew over the ugly sisters plunged out of the sky—clay pigeons felled by their own curiosity. Perseus took his direction from the distant thud and crack of breaking vultures and by the sight of them plummeting out of the sky a league away.

He flew over an oasis, and there below him a woman was combing her hair, using a pool of water for her mirror. All of a sudden, the woman dropped her comb with a splash and stared up: she had caught sight in the pool of the reflection of a young man flying overhead.

"By Zeus! By Athene! By all the gods!" cried Perseus, somersaulting through the air. "Would it work? Could it work?"

He thought of turning back and asking the Nymphs, but would they know? He considered retracing his steps and asking the gray-eyed Graeae, but he knew they would only lie to him. He called out to the gods, "Will it work? Will it work?" But there was no answering sound except the shriek and crack of vultures thudding to Earth half a league away. There was only one way of finding out if his idea would work: he would have to try.

He practiced over the desert sands. Flying on his back like a swimmer saving the life of a drowning friend, he held the shield over his head and stared into the reflection on its inside. The hollow curve made everything reflected in it look smaller, farther off. But he could see the waves of sand speckled by stones, the lizards running to and fro, the spiny fruit of the cactus as red as a man's heart. He put on the Helmet of Invisibility and became no more than a flash of light, a streak of whiteness, a brightness too bright to see.

"Before I was born it was decided," said Perseus aloud to himself, "whether I shall kill Medusa or Medusa will kill me. My fate is already written in the brain of the oracles of the world, and no wishing will change it. So let's find out what the Fates have in store for me!" He rolled onto his back and held the shield over him; it shielded him from the great heat of the noonday and it reflected

every spiky shrub, every scorpion, every beetle and but-
terfly below him.

The Gorgons lolled, flaccid and fleshy, among the rocky
remains of their victims. Their soft rolls of fatness were
piled up round their feet, and their stumpy wings
drooped from fleshy shoulder blades. Their horrible
claws crammed pebbles and guano into their tusked
mouths, and between mouthfuls their tongues hung out
over their double chins, drooling repulsively. Like the
thrums of a rug, green snakes coiled densely out of their
bony skulls and tasted the air, first one way then another,
with forked, flickering tongues. Some short, some long,
they knotted and writhed and hissed, and now and
then the Gorgons scratched in among them with a piece
of stick.

"You're looking older today, Sister," said Euryale with
a sneer.

"So? So what if I am?" retorted Medusa. "I'll have to
grow a lot older before I'm as ugly as either of you!" But
the anger rising through her veins made the snakes on
her head break out in a deafening hiss. She hated her
sisters when they reminded her that they were immortal,
whereas she must grow older and older and one day die.
"You're only jealous!" she taunted them. "Just because I
was loved once. Just because Poseidon gave me his—"
But she broke off, because a crawling of her infested
scalp told her that something warm-blooded and alive

was close at hand. "Who is it? Who's there?" The snakes tossed and groped upward from her head, but neither they nor she could see anything—only sense a closeness, a dangerous closeness.

Medusa shielded her eyes with her small, fat claws and looked up at the empty sky. But it was noon, and she was dazzled; the sun left marks on her eyes like little sword cuts. Her flat gray nose smelled human flesh, even so. "Sisters! Sisters! Is someone coming? Is someone close at hand? Why doesn't it turn to stone? And why can't I see it? Oh, Poseidon, is it you come back to me? Are you playing a trick on me, my lover?"

Reflected on the inside of his shield, Perseus saw below him the cairns of rock that had once been men and women. He saw the rags of clothing still blowing round them, the looks of fear fixed forever in stone. Then he saw a green-clawed foot and the feathers of a stubby wing and a roll of flesh and a green strand of seeming hair . . . and then at last three faces looking up to search the sky.

He felt his blood run cold. He felt the hairs on his arms and neck lift and prickle. He felt his own face go gray—a ghastly gray as all the blood fled out of his lips and cheeks. Had his ruse not worked, then? "Is that my fate?" he asked himself. "Is this how it feels to be turned to stone?"

But his heart kept pounding and his hand kept hold of the shield and his eyes went on seeing—though it was a sight almost too loathsome to bear—the three crouched shapes of the Gorgons. He drew his curved sickle sword. He feathered his flight. He sank low over the hideous sisters—straight out of the dazzle of the noonday sun.

But which was Medusa? He had only one chance to guess right, for if he hacked at the neck of the immortal Stheno or Euryale, they would drag him out of the air. The snakes could sense him: they groped toward him, they strained in their bony sockets to reach up and pierce him with poisonous fangs. He lay in the air above them as close as a swimmer to the thick, green weed of a riverbed; his back was almost brushing them. But which was Medusa?

"MEDUSA!" he shouted at the top of his voice, and it seemed to him that one face turned before the rest. He dropped the dark cloth bag over that one (like the hangman's blindfold), and that was where he let his curved sword fall.

It is difficult, in a mirror, to tell left from right, to judge distances, to aim a blow. Medusa spread her wings and threw up her arms to tear free the bag covering her head. One hand struck Perseus and knocked off the Helmet of Invisibility. But the sword of Hermes fell as true as a beam of sun. And when Perseus pulled tight the cords of the black bag and clambered up through the scream-filled air, the bag weighed heavy and jerked in his grasp.

To Euryale and Stheno, Perseus seemed to materialize

out of the very air over their heads: one moment there was no one, the next there was this bird-man shouting a name, loosing a sword stroke. They lunged and they clawed, but all they found in their grip was a tuft from the crest of a helmet and a scrap of cloth from a tunic.

When they saw the swaying stump of their sister—like a tree struck by lightning—they let out such a screech of grief and rage that several of the stony figures shivered into sand then and there. The immortal Gorgons spread their dirty wings and beat the air so hard that it must have bruised. Ponderously, they lifted their great weights into the air and took off in pursuit of Medusa's murderer.

Chapter Six

Winged Pegasus

ALL THAT WAS left of Medusa rocked on its clawlike feet—like a volcano after the Earth's core has blasted off its peak and left only a gaping crater red, red, red with welling magma.

Just as the blood flowing from a cut will flow until it has cleansed the wound, so Medusa bled until out of her body was washed something: something white, something huge, something shapeless and lumpen slumped onto the ground. It was as brilliant a white as ocean spray. Little wonder, for it was the child conceived by Medusa in her days of beauty—the child of the Earth-Shaker, the Earthquake-Maker, Poseidon, god of the sea. It was a horse.

And yet it was not a horse, for lying along its back, gradually breaking, unfolding, spreading, flapping, two immense wings rose up until their topmost feathers met. Unstained by his mother's blood, Pegasus the Winged Horse was born, as wild as temper.

His shadow fell huge on the Libyan sands, then only

as large as an eagle, then only as small as a hawk, as Pegasus leaped higher and higher into the sky, snaking his white neck, flaring his dark nostrils, and trampling the air with his white hoofs. Foam spumed from his lips and flecked all his sweating neck and flanks, and his eyes rolled in a vengeful frenzy.

The two Gorgons, for all their stumpy wings, were so enraged by the murder of their sister that they kept pace with Perseus, who dared not look back over his shoulder. He was unaccustomed to flying, and his limbs were tired with struggling to keep his balance in the air. Once, twice he stumbled into a somersault, pitching end over end. Behind him he could hear the Gorgon sisters shriek with triumphant, joyless laughter and gain on him a little. The pack with Medusa's head in it weighed heavy as a boulder; he feared the black cloth must split and let fall his trophy, but it only banged, banged against his thigh. He had thought the writhing of the snakes inside was a simple reflex—like chickens who go on running about after their heads are cut off. He expected that one by one they would wilt and die. But the snakes did not die at all; their hissing went on as loud as ever.

And that was not all that escaped the bag. Seeping through the black cloth, Medusa's blood dripped, dripped onto the desert below. And as each gout of blood touched the ground, it bored a deep, small hole in the sand. A moment later, out of each hole wriggled a green serpent, its fangs charged with a deadly venom.

The blood of Medusa seeded the world's deserts with snakes.

The rhythmic beat of the white horse's wings seemed to be counting away Perseus's life in seconds—five, four, three, two—as with each stride it gained on him.

"Kill, horse! Kill!" shrieked the Gorgons. "Bite him! Trample him! Kick him! Ride him down! Ride him down!"

A shadow fell on Perseus as the horse leaped over him and cut off the sunlight. The boy saw the hoofs falling on him. He pulled in his head and heels and tumbled through the air so that Pegasus completely overshot him. But now he was trapped between horse and Gorgons. He flew back the way he had come, holding his shield in front of him so as not to see the hideous sisters. What if their gaze, too, could turn a man to rock? Then Perseus would fall like a meteorite to the ground and become just one more boulder in a desert of boulders.

So intent was he on not seeing the Gorgons that he collided with Euryale in midair. There was a squeal and a grunt, and two hooked hands came round the edge of the shield and pulled it downward. And there he was, face to face with that snout, those tusks, that great lolling tongue. His despair gave Perseus a superhuman strength, and he wrenched free his shield. But though his blood ran as cold as meltwater and his flesh crawled, he did not turn to stone at the sight of Euryale or the smell of her foul breath. She struck out at him with the thing she happened to be holding in her claw—his own magic

Helmet. In fending off the blow, he raised the sickle sword, and its wire-sharp blade cut through the chin strap of the Helmet and brought it crashing into his face. Somehow, with the back of a hand, with the rim of the shield, he crammed it onto his head—just as Stheno flew up beneath him and snatched at his winged feet.

He felt their touch—it was scaly and dry like a crocodile and grazed his skin. But a moment later—when they might have torn him in two between them—they were bawling and brawling with each other. "Where did he go?" "What have you done with him?" "Did he melt? Did we dream him?" "No! I can smell him still!"

The invisible Perseus half swam, half flew out of their reach. A whooping triumph swelled in his throat, and he wanted to laugh at their squabbling and taunt them. But as he went to put away his sickle sword, a blow in his back knocked all the breath out of him in a pained, panicked cry. Pegasus, startled by his invisible foe and maddened by the scent of him, flailed at the air with his front hoofs and snapped with his long, white teeth.

The only safe place in all the wide skies seemed to be astride the beast's back. And that was where Perseus found himself. He flung Athene's shield across his back, he crammed the Helmet of Invisibility down so hard onto his skull that he could barely see out, and he pushed the sickle sword through his belt. Then he clung on grimly with both hands and both knees. The bag containing Medusa's head thumped into the animal's white ribs, and winged Pegasus felt for the first time in his short life what it was to be ridden by a man.

He took off at a gallop that set Perseus and his baggage clattering. The Gorgon sisters, by the time they realized what was happening, could only pant and grunt after the shrinking speck of white, until it disappeared over the horizon. All that remained of their sister was a trail of wriggling serpents on the desert below.

Pegasus bucked and reared, stretched round and bit, but nothing would dislodge the rider from his back. He was so intent on the struggle that he failed to notice the vast barrier of a mountain rising up into the sky ahead of him.

The gods lining the parapets of heaven to watch had a marvelous view. For Pegasus was flying directly toward Mount Olympus, his great wings cutting elegant sweeps through the air, his head turned away to snap at his invisible rider. (To the gods, of course, nothing is invisible.)

"Here they come!"

"What a horse!"

"Isn't that your shield, Athene?"

"Isn't that your sword, Hermes?"

"Aren't they your sandals . . . ?"

"Look out!"

"I say, have a care!"

Suddenly the sleepy, languid gods were scattering to left and right; some dived to the floor; some were bowled onto their backs as Pegasus, mindless of the mountain in his way, flew straight into it, pulling up his head only at the last moment. His hoofs clipped the escarpment.

And where they did so, a redness spurted out. Perseus saw it and exclaimed, "What? Now even the world is bleeding! Can cliffs bleed?"

It was not blood at all. Pegasus, having sweated himself to a parching thirst, flew in a circle and paused to drink at the red, welling stream now cascading down Olympus's cliffside. He drank and snickered and staggered and rose up again on lopsided wings.

When he had gone, the gods hurried down as fast as dignity would allow, and dabbed at the stream with their fingers. They scooped up the red liquor in their palms. They stained their robes reaching for more.

"Look! It's all running down to Earth," said one. "We should dam it up. This is too good for the little mortals down there—too strong for their silly little brains." But somehow the dam was never built, and the wine continued to flow from the highest slopes of Olympus, down through the vineyards of Greece. Hippocrene, "wine-of-the-horse," they called it, and gods and men delighted in it equally, though it made them all as drunk as ticks.

Having drunk a gallon of Hippocrene, Pegasus mellowed. The animal sagged at the shoulders and lowered his lids against the brightness of the sinking sun. Horse and rider sank down into the long shadows of Africa.

•   •   •

In Africa there stood, in those days, a man more bent at the shoulder, more heavy at heart than even King Acrisius of Argos. His lot in life was dreadful: to hold up the sky forever and to keep it from crashing onto the Earth beneath. The icy clouds buffeted his face and the birds perched in the corner of his eye and eagles nested in his cavernous ears. But when the sun glared in his face or the flinty stars drove their sharp points into his bent neck, he could not fend off the pain, for his hands were everlastingly spread to support the level sky. Just once he had known a moment's relief when Hercules the Strong had taken his place in return for a favor. But Hercules had tricked Atlas back into his never-ending ordeal.

Heavy as the heavens were, there was something heavier still that Atlas had to bear. It was the fear of his fate. For an oracle had prophesied Atlas would lose his life one day at the hands of a son of Zeus.

"How can I die when I'm immortal?" Atlas had demanded, half scoffing, half angry. But no answer came to his question, and at length fear took the place of scorn and anger. Fear gnawed away at Atlas's heart as it gnawed at the heart of King Acrisius. Only one emotion was stronger than the fear. Standing in that one remote spot, unable to move and surrounded by dark, trackless Africa, Atlas was as lonely as One.

Perseus and Pegasus landed late in the gloomy evening. Both were as exhausted as each other. Perseus took off his Helmet and wiped his face.

"By Zeus! That was clever! Where did you spring from?"

Pegasus pranced and bucked and rolled his white lips back off his white teeth at the sound of the booming voice. Perseus snatched out his sickle sword. "Who's there? Show yourself!"

"Look up, young man. You are camped in the lee of my left leg. No call to disturb yourself. I never sit down. But if you would care to move round to the front, it might be easier to talk. I'd be heartily glad of your news, young fellow. You are most welcome to my humble realm. My name is Atlas."

"I've heard of you!" exclaimed Perseus, suddenly wide awake. "Your hospitality is famous throughout the world!"

"Is it? Is it indeed? How pleasant. How very nice to know. Do feel free to light a campfire. I can provide a bird or two from my humble larder." And he swatted a pair of songbirds that had been singing overloud in his ear. The sky tilted momentarily, and a sprinkling of stars fell.

While Pegasus slept, Perseus built a fire and cooked himself some supper and entertained Atlas with the story of his quest for the head of Medusa.

"And you mean to say that you—a small mortal from Seriphus—have cut off Medusa's head?"

Perseus smiled rather smugly. "I do believe I had a little help from the gods." He showed the shield and the sickle sword and the bag. Atlas looked doubtful.

"Why should they help you? No offense, boy—but why

exactly should the gods take it into their heads to help some penniless boy with the smell of fish on his hands? Show me the head. Go on. Show me. I daresay you've been killing lizards or lopping willow trees."

Perseus was not offended. A cocksure arrogance was stirring in him—the one that had made him promise Medusa's head to King Polydectes in the first place. He felt about him in the darkness for the pack. (If it was hard to see in the daylight, it was impossible to find in the dark.) "My mother has often told me the story of how I came to be born. And it seems to me—though I can't quite work out the way of it—that my father must be one of the gods themselves." He laughed at a sudden extravagant idea: "Maybe even Zeus himself!" His hands still mislaid the nasty, writhing bag in among the long grass.

"Liar! Liar!" bawled Atlas, kicking out at Perseus and scattering the campfire in a flurry of sparks. The sky quaked like the skin of a drum, and the echo ricocheted between ground and cloud, plain and planets. "Liar-iar-iar!"

Bowled head over heels by the kick, his arm over his head to protect him from the earsplitting noise, Perseus was too startled to cry out.

"YOU? You worm! You squirt! You braggart! You, the son of Zeus? Ha! I laugh at the idea, see? Ha-ha!" Atlas was leaning down so low that the whole pallet of the sky on his back sloped at a dangerous angle and planets slid into unlucky alignments and the stars jostled. "Get off

61

my land! Get out of my realm, you boasting whelp, or I'll kick you all the way from here to the Hesperides! You're a boasting storyteller! Your father's some sailor who took your mother's fancy—some beggar, some wretch, some dwarf. . . ." Perseus could see Atlas's eyes, large as moons, bulging with rage. They reflected a few red sparks from the scattered fire.

"Is this the famous hospitality you show your guests?" cried Perseus, but his voice was choked with amazement and drowned out by Atlas howling, "Liar! Liar! LIAR!"

"And I say I *am* the son of Zeus. How else would I have killed the Gorgon?" The clouds were shaken clear of the moon, and Perseus could at last fumble his way to the lost black bag. It wriggled under his touch. He pulled open the cords and, holding the bag from underneath so that the cloth fell back over his hand and arm, held up Medusa's head. "See it for yourself, if you don't believe me!"

Atlas stared.

He is staring now. Although his staring eyes you might mistake for white scars on a hillside and his gaping mouth for a cave. You might take his hair for a plantation of trees and his bent back for the bare upper slopes of a mountain range. For Atlas was turned to rock by the son of Zeus.

His bones are buried deep now—like strata of rock.

Loose earth blown in on the wind buried him, and grass took root in the earth and blurred every sharpness—his elbow, his knees, his heel, his jaw. . . .

Clouds covered the moon again. In the darkness, Perseus could not tell what had happened. One moment Atlas had been towering over him, raging, shouting, deafening him with insults. Now the African night was quiet. The smell of sweaty giant was gone. After a few seconds, the chirruping roar of insects filled up the silence. Somewhere, a wild animal howled. The horse Pegasus, so white that he glowed in the dark, woke up and pawed the ground in an ecstasy of nervousness.

Perseus thrust Medusa's head back into its pack without looking at it. He was disappointed that Atlas had (apparently) stormed off without bothering to see the convincing proof of Perseus's heroism. But it was also a relief not to have to fight the giant. After all, the man was as big as a mountain!

He picked up all his bits and pieces of baggage and leaped astride the winged horse once more, before Pegasus could bolt for freedom or remember his hatred toward Perseus. Up among the stars, riding out the tantrum that followed, Perseus came to the conclusion that this steed of his might be a little on the stupid side. Tantrums are often the last resort of the stupid.

Chapter Seven

Two More Visitors for the Oracle

THE RUINS OF the old tower were falling! His legs would not carry him out of the way! First single bricks, then whole sections of wall, wooden beams, iron window bars, winches, a little bed, and table all hurtled down on him, burying him alive. He tried to cry out, but his mouth filled up with dusty mortar. Then the whole tower, with infinite slowness, keeled over and fell on him so that no amount of digging would ever rescue him from under the rubble.

King Acrisius woke up screaming and threw off his bedclothes as though they were crushing the life out of him. Wiping the sweat from his face with a pillow, he went to the window and looked out. The tower had long since been pulled down, of course—immediately after the first nightmare he had given the order for it to be razed to the ground. But the bad dreams went on, night after night.

Could that be what the oracle had meant? That little Perseus—little drowned Perseus, little dead and drowned

Perseus—would leave behind him such nightmares as to stop up Acrisius's thumping heart?

Or was he not really dead at all? Had Acrisius's daughter and grandson really sunk and drowned in that leaky chest? He imagined them still down there after eighteen years, holding their breath.

For eighteen years? No! It was impossible! Danaë and Perseus had not lived so much as an hour. . . . Well, not so much as a day . . .

Perhaps a week, if the chest had floated . . .

And if it had floated, might not some ship's captain have seen it and taken it aboard and smashed the lock and found . . . ? Acrisius shuddered with a sudden cold.

"Boy! Boy, where are you?" His page tottered into the room dizzy with sleep. "Tell the stables to make ready a chariot. I must go to Epidaurus."

"Now, Sire? In the middle of the—"

"Now!" And Acrisius threw the pillow he was clutching, though it missed the boy and only toppled a valuable, carved bust of the king. The sculpture fell onto the marble floor, and the hollow head shattered.

Acrisius thought he could see loathing in the eyes of the oracle at Epidaurus. He was wrong. Oracles have no feelings. But Acrisius tended to see loathing in every pair of eyes that looked at him. It was only the reflection of his own guilt.

"What is-s it this-s-s time, Acris-s-ius-s-s?" hissed the oracle.

The king's voice was shrill and loud with hysteria. "I just came to tell you you were wrong! You were, weren't you? Admit it. You were wrong!"

"I am never wrong," said the oracle, turning away its hooded head, "and fate is unchangeable."

"So-ho! Tell me now that Perseus is going to kill me! You can't, eh, can you? You can't, see!"

"Pers-seus-s-s is going to kill you, Acris-sius-s-s," said the oracle implacably. "You may go now."

"But I—"

"You what, Acris-sius-s-s?" said the oracle, without the smallest note of curiosity. "I s-s-see blood on your hands-s, s-ssir. Bes-st go home and wash-sh-sh it off."

Acrisius snatched his hands back inside the sleeves of his robe and rushed outside, his diaphragm quaking with horror. In the daylight he was mightily relieved to see that the redness in his palms was only where he had clenched his fists so tight that his nails had cut the skin and made it bleed. Dreadful if the oracle had meant something else . . .

"But I didn't murder anyone!" he blurted out loud. "I just put them in a chest."

So perhaps they were not dead.

"But they must be dead. I killed them!" Try as he might, Acrisius could not make up his mind which was true, which he wanted to be true. He went home and commissioned spies to keep watch the world over for news of his dead daughter and his dead grandson.

After he had gone, the oracle had a second visitor.

"Two kings-s in one day," observed the serpent, and a slight sneer creased the hard rim of its mouth. "What do you want, Cepheus-s-s?"

King Cepheus, who had come in disguise with his hood pulled far forward over his face, sat down sharply on the floor; his legs trembled too much to hold him. He had a horror of snakes.

"A friend of mine has a problem," he began.

"Come, come, Cepheus-s-s. Don't ins-sult my intelligence-ce. Friend, indeed. You wish-sh to know how to be rid of your s-s-sea mons-s-ster." In the oracle's mouth, the beast's name seemed as long as its body.

"Yes-s-s . . . I mean 'yes,'" said Cepheus, trying not to catch sight of the weaving, waving head or the flickering fangs.

"Why did Pos-seidon s-send it agains-s-s-t you?" asked the creature, although the question sounded like a statement.

Cepheus answered in a guilty rush. "Because my foolish wife bragged that our daughter was more beautiful than the mermaids. And those vicious women—fish—what is a mermaid, exactly?"

"A mammal," said the oracle, yawning.

"Well then, those vicious mammals went whining to

67

Poseidon, and he took a piece of this and a bit of that and molded it all together into . . . into . . . well, you've seen it, haven't you? There, inside your head? It's hideous!"

The oracle ducked down and poked its green head round Cepheus's hand to stare him in the eye. "Because it is-s s-so very s-s-serpentlike?" hissed the serpent menacingly.

Cepheus gave a scream and cowered backward. "Not at all! No! But it keeps eating things, doesn't it? Goats and pigs and sheep and cows and horses. And last night it pushed down a wall and walked through the streets of Ammon. For the love of the gods! What must I do to save my kingdom?"

There was a long, terrible silence before the serpent said, "Why did you was-ste time traveling here, Cepheus-s? You know full well what s-s-sacrifice you mus-s-s-t make."

"No! NO! Not Andromeda! Not my daughter! Not my lovely, innocent daughter! Not her! Have pity, won't you? Say my wife! Say my prime minister—I wouldn't mind that! But not Andromeda! Her marriage is all arranged! There must be some other way!"

The oracle stared at the ceiling until King Cepheus had shouted himself silent. "I promis-se you this-s-s, Cepheus-s-s: Andromeda will never marry Agenor. That is-s not her fate. Deck her with jewels-s, then chain her to the flat, black rock by the s-sea. You know the one.

Andromeda is-s the only apology Pos-seidon will accept for the ins-sult to his mermaids-s-s. It is-s her fate."

A week later, the Princess Andromeda sat at the family dinner table, along with her betrothed, the handsome Prince Agenor, and wondered at her parents' strange behavior. First her father had presented her with a necklace and a belt of the most exquisite lapis lazuli set in gold. Now her mother was sobbing silently into her sleeve ends. They both sat stabbing the food on their plates as though it had done them an injury. And neither spoke, though Agenor leaped up from time to time to look out of the windows. He swore he could hear the sea monster scratching at the city wall.

"What are you going to do about it, father-in-law-to-be?" he asked in his sharp, nasal voice. "I have to tell you, it's very difficult indeed to organize the wedding—everyone is so nervous of the wretched beast. And I do hate to see darling Andromeda so anxious. And there's so little food! I thought I'd wear my purple. What do you think, dearest? It suits me well, doesn't it?"

"Yes, Agenor. It suits you very well," whispered Andromeda, her thoughts taken up with her parents' odd behavior. "You still haven't said, Father. Did the oracle know a way to be rid of the sea monster?"

King Cepheus choked on a mouthful of bread, and his daughter had to bang him on the back. He caught hold of her hands for a moment, then let go as if her fingers were too hot to touch. "Yes, Andromeda. The oracle knew what must be done."

"Excellent!" declared Agenor, draping the curtain over one shoulder to see if the color suited him. "We'll have the wedding the day after it's done. I thought we'd have sports afterward, to entertain the guests. Have you ever seen me throw a discus, my dearest darling Andromeda?" He picked up a plate and seemed about to demonstrate, but Andromeda gently took it away from him and put it back on the table.

"Tell us, Father. Will it be very difficult?"

Cepheus covered his face with his hands. "Yes, Daughter, it will be the most difficult thing I've ever done." And pulling his robe over his face, he rapped three times on the table.

Suddenly armed soldiers leaped into the room at every door and window—big, ungentle men with necks as broad as their shaven heads and arms covered in battle scars. One seized Andromeda from behind, pinning her arms to her sides in a fierce embrace.

"I say!" protested Agenor. "Let go of my dear darling betrothed!"

The king and queen fled the room, colliding at the doorway and struggling with each other to be out of the sight of their betrayed daughter. "I'm sorry! I'm sorry! I'm sorry! It's all your mother's fault!" wailed Cepheus over his shoulder, and Queen Cassiopeia shouted and slapped at him in bitter denial. "She has to die, Agenor!"

cried Cepheus. "The oracle says so! It's her fate! She has to be chained to a rock to feed the sea monster! The mermaids demand it! Forgive us, boy. Forgive us, Andromeda! Forgive us!" His footsteps pattered away along the echoing corridor pursued by the queen's sobbing.

In the soldier's arms Andromeda stopped struggling and stared after them, breathing fast and shallow. Then she turned her eyes to Agenor whose sword was half out of its sheath. "Will you let them do this to me?" she pleaded.

The sword slid home again with a thud. "Poor dear darling Andromeda," he said flatly.

The soldier lifted Andromeda as though she were a piece of army baggage. "Help me, Agenor! You won't let them feed me to the monster! I know you won't! Not you! Not if you love me!"

"Ah." Agenor studied the sleeve of his robe and, with extreme concentration, began to pick at a blob of candle wax, which had stained it. "Well, if it really is the only way to satisfy the horrible thing . . ."

"Agenor! Help me!" Her hands reached out toward him as the soldier carried her out into the gardens. A host of butterflies flew up off the bushes and flowers. "AGENOR!"

Her young man hurried down the seaward path after his betrothed and the squad of brutal soldiers. He raised his voice and called, "It's a terrific honor for you, of course, dearest! I only wish it were my fate to save Ammon from

71

the sea monster! People will always be grateful to you after this! And if the oracle says it's your fate, who am I to argue?"

"Agenor, I hate you!"

"Now, now. You don't mean that. Think about it. It's an immense honor, if you'll just think about it . . . and I'm sure the unpleasant part will be over very quickly. . . ."

"Mother! Father! Agenor!"

The chains hung waiting from the smooth black rock by the seashore—high up to fasten her wrists and low down for her ankles. As Agenor's high-pitched voice droned on at a distance—"an honor really . . . a very great public service . . ."—the bull-necked soldier manacled her with the iron rings. Then he pinned her to the rock with his shoulder while he put the tip of his sword to her delicate robe and slit it from throat to hem. The two pieces fell away into the eager, gaping sea and left her in only the necklace and belt of lapis lazuli and gold.

At the sight of this, Agenor's voice died in his throat, and he covered his face with his hands and stumbled away up the cliff path whimpering, ". . . soon be over . . . soon be over."

"Sorry about him," said the soldier gruffly. "No loss as a husband, that one." His stubbly, scarred cheeks were red with blushes. Both he and Andromeda watched her torn, white robe wash to and fro in the water before it sank slowly out of sight. "Orders, see. Orders . . . Well. I'd . . . er . . . I must be going, Lady. Good luck."

A wave broke against the rocky platform, and they were both deluged in bitter spray. "I'm afraid you must be awful cold, Lady. I hope the sea monster won't be long in coming."

"If I were your daughter . . . if I were your wife . . . would you leave me here to die such a death?" pleaded Andromeda.

"Fate's fate, Lady. There's no changing that." His nervous glances said that he expected the sea monster at any moment to lurch up out of the water at their feet. He sheathed his sword, saluted her once, and hurried back up the cliff path in awkward leaping strides. Andromeda's head sank onto her chest, and her yellow hair, spilling down her body, clung to her spray-wet skin.

As far away as a migrating bird, Perseus rode Pegasus across a cloudless sky. The winged horse had not given in to its rider, but it was stupid, easily fooled, and Perseus had only to put on his Helmet of Invisibility to catch and mount the beast whenever he wanted.

Below him, the sea was an amazement of different colors. Shoals of krill, rafts of seaweed, underwater reefs, and eddies of surface wind made patches of green, white, and turquoise. Dolphins left dotted trails, and flying fishes burst like fireworks into the air. Diving gulls pelted the water, and the dark shapes of sunken ships lay whirled round with bright shoals of fish.

He thought the sea monster, too, was a ship's hulk

until, with a flick of its tail, it moved off in lazy undulations through the water below him. The glare off the waves smudged its shape and color. He did not see clearly its barnacle-encrusted back, its hooked fins, its banks of jagged teeth, the fronded, raggy barbules that waved round its massive, dewlapped mouth, nor the six legs that dangled from its scaly underbelly. He wondered that there could be such strange beasts in the world. But moving far faster than any waterborne creature could swim, Perseus overtook the cruising monster and flew on in hope of sighting land. He was unsure where he was and which way he ought to be flying.

"I trust in the gods to direct me," he said out loud, his face cocked toward the sky. But there were few gods available to see or hear him at that particular moment.

Most of those on Olympus had gone down to Africa to see if the rumors were true—that the immortal Atlas had been turned into a mountain by a teenage boy with a clutter of magic baggage.

Chapter Eight

Love at First Sight

AT FIRST SHE was nothing more than a patch of white and gold and flashing lapis lazuli, seen out of the corner of his eye. Even when he came closer, he did not quite believe what his eyes were telling him—that someone had chained this beautiful young woman to a rock to be splashed by the angry sea. It was Pegasus who decided the matter, settling down onto the slippery platform to drink from a rock pool.

At the sound of the horse's clattering hoofs and fanning wings, Andromeda, who had her eyes tight shut and her hair over her face, began to scream and scream and scream.

With an angry flick of his sensitive ears, Pegasus wandered off along the shore and left Perseus standing dumbfounded on the sacrificial platform of black granite. Remembering his manners at last, he quickly removed the Helmet of Invisibility and put it under his arm. It left him no hands free to cover his ears; he did wish she would stop screaming. "Please don't alarm yourself, Madam. My horse is unpleasant but remarkably stupid."

75

Andromeda's eyes opened, wide and round as whirl-pools . . . and Perseus was sucked in and lost everlastingly in fathoms of love.

"Your horse?" she said. "Who are you?"

"Were you expecting someone else? I'm sorry. I'll go."

"Don't go," said Andromeda hastily.

It was difficult for Perseus to know what to say. He had never seen a naked woman chained to a rock before. He looked at his feet for lack of knowing where else to look. "Aren't you rather cold?"

"Perished," said Andromeda.

"You're extraordinarily beautiful, if you don't mind me saying so."

"Come back tomorrow. You won't think so then," said Andromeda.

"I could stand here and look at you forever." Having dared to glance at her face, he could not now unfix his eyes.

"Then you would be eaten, too, and I'm sure I don't wish that on anyone," said Andromeda.

"Eaten?"

"Why do you suppose I'm standing here, young man?" she asked irritably. "In other circumstances I might enjoy talking to you, but I have a great deal on my mind just at the moment. Must you stare so at my jewels?"

"What jewels?" said Perseus. "What do you mean, 'eaten'?"

So Andromeda explained how her mother had bragged, how the mermaids had taken offense, how Poseidon had assembled the monster, how the oracle had spoken her fate. The waves broke tediously up against the rock, and they were both wet through before she had done.

"I think that's the saddest story I ever heard," said Perseus, wiping salt water off his cheek with the heel of his hand.

"I'm so glad you enjoyed it."

"And this sea monster is due here shortly?"

"Any moment."

"Then I'd best hurry. Which way is your parents' palace?"

"Why? Do you want supper?" she hissed, straining forward from the rock though it twisted her arms in their sockets.

"No. No time. I just want to be sure they'll let me marry you if I kill this sea monster. . . . You wouldn't mind, would you? Marrying me, I mean? Only I've been in love with you ever since I laid eyes on you, and my mother said that if I ever loved a woman I ought to marry her before anything else. Unlike my father, you know. Whoever he was. You see—"

"Sir!" said Andromeda. "I would marry your horse if it saved me from being eaten! You don't have to ask my mother and father! I'll marry you! I'll marry you!"

While Perseus pondered this, a large wave slopped over his feet and made the wings on his sandals sodden. "No, no. I think I really must ask your mother and father for permission. Mother told me if I met a woman I loved, I must ask the blessing of her mother and father. Unlike my father. You see—"

"SIR!"

He was loath to stop looking at her, but at last tore himself away and set off up the path to the royal palace. "Oh, I forgot! I should lend you my cloak!" he called back.

"LATER!"

"Oh, and I'm very honored that you're willing to marry me."

Andromeda did not answer. Winged Pegasus had wandered back along the beach and was licking her thoughtfully with his long, rasping tongue, savoring the salty taste of her skin.

When he finally found King Cepheus and Queen Cassiopeia, they seemed very pleased with the idea of Perseus marrying their daughter. They were scornful at first, until he told them he had just beheaded Medusa. Then they could not promise their blessing quickly enough. Perseus was quite flushed with pleasure. "At home they call me One-shirt Perseus," he said.

King Cepheus stood holding the door open. "You're welcome. You're welcome. Now go and fight the sea monster! Please!"

"Of course it's most selfish of me to want to marry a princess when I have no money to buy her clothes or feed her on anything but bread and sardines. . . ."

"He wants money," said the queen, grabbing her husband's sleeve. "Promise him money, Cepheus. Promise him anything."

"Oh, I didn't mean—"

"Half my kingdom!" cried King Cepheus falling on his knees in front of Perseus. "Half my kingdom is yours if you kill the sea monster and save Andromeda!"

"Oh, I—"

"But do HURRY! The monster comes at sunset, and the sun is already dipping into the sea! Go! Go! Go!"

Perseus rearranged all his baggage—his shield and pack and sword and helmet—and hovered away across the garden, disturbing the butterflies for a second time that day. In the distant sea, a dark shape was cutting its way inshore through the smooth, gleaming swell, along the scarlet path of the setting sun. For a moment it looked as though Poseidon's monster were swimming in blood.

At the sight of the monster watching her from among the waves, Andromeda fainted. The beast was transfixed; the answer to its longings was suddenly there. It had been formed and made to hunger after Andromeda. As Poseidon took a piece of alligator, a shred of shark, a morsel of whale, a section of moray eel, and molded his ravenous, vengeful monster, he poured into its sea-cold blood all the heat he had felt for Medusa, all the hunger he still felt for beauty, all the violence he normally reserved for causing tidal waves and earthquakes. So the monster thought and dreamed and pictured and bayed for Andromeda. And when it found her staked out as a gift, its ecstasy was horrible to see. It leaped and pranced in the sea, and its tongue lolled out through its thousands of teeth. Its nostrils were full of her sweet smell. It scraped its clawed fins on the shallowing seabed and stretched out its neck. . . .

A dart of light glimpsed out of the corner of its eye was all that the monster saw of Perseus. But at the first clash of the sickle sword across its steely neck, the monster threw up its head and sent its attacker tumbling through the air. The Helmet of Invisibility fell into the sea; the pack holding Medusa's head dropped, too, into a bed of seaweed, and the shallow water closed over it. Perseus steadied himself, his winged feet trailing in the surf, then pitched himself at the monster, striking with sword and shining shield.

The beast was enraged at being kept from its sweet, delicious prey. But Perseus, having lost Medusa's head, was every bit as angry. He rained blows on the monstrous snout, and teeth rattled into the sea. But the scales of its skin were tougher than leather, and the lash of its tail quick to find its mark. It coiled round Perseus and held him underwater until he thought his lungs had turned to stone inside him.

At last the creature brought its captive close to its mouth to rend him in its teeth. Then Perseus was able not only to snatch a breath of air but to jab the tip of his sickle sword into the lolling, pink tongue. The beast loosed an earsplitting whistle through its gills and, throwing Perseus aside in disgust, turned back toward its chief prey—Andromeda.

Its stumpy alligator legs mounted the platform of black rock and began to pull the rest of its long body up out of the water. Perseus—his shield gone now and floating like a bright reflection on top of the waves— swam with his sword in his fist and pulled himself astride the broad, finny back. The beast lost its hold, and they both slid off the rock and under the water, where they rolled over and over and over in a deadly embrace. Perseus cut himself on his own sword and on the sharp scales of the monster; pain and the smell of human blood drove the creature to a greater madness. The nasty fronded feelers round its mouth sucked and groped at Perseus's head, and the gills opened and closed in panting, evil-smelling breaths. Through the gill flaps Perseus drove in his sword, and with one more massive shudder that threatened to pin the boy against the black rocky cliff, Poseidon's sea monster went suddenly limp.

As flaccid and buoyant as a dead whale, it lolled in the water, feet uppermost, only its heavy skull resting on the seabed. Perseus pulled himself onto the sharp-edged platform of rock and lay like a man dead at Andromeda's feet.

"My hero!" she said, reviving. "I love you. But who are you?"

"Perseus," he replied, squeezing the seawater out of his golden hair. "And I love you, too."

When he went to gather up his belongings, the shield had beached itself like a little round boat. The pack containing Medusa's head he never expected to find, for it had fallen in among the waving, rust-red fronds of a thousand sea anemones and a forest of seaweed. But when he swam to where he had seen it fall, he barked his knees on a sharpness and cut razory slashes in the soles of his sandals as he stood up on the shallow, solid stuff. It was red still—as blood-red as the anemones had been—but was as brittle now as shale or flint. It was weirdly beautiful, but dead, and the bag rested on top of this delicate reef, within ready reach of Perseus's dipping hand.

A singularly unpleasant thought crept into his mind as he slung the pack across his shoulder and the head banged against the small of his back. He began to realize that Medusa's magic was still seeping out of this nasty trophy of his: a magic that could turn living things to stone.

They called it coral, afterward—that brilliant, blood-red, brittle, shining, stony stuff. Its beauty made it precious, and it was prized by mermaids and princesses alike.

As for Pegasus, he was nowhere to be found. He had seized the chance for freedom, catching the warm noon breezes under his wings and losing his whiteness among canyons of creamy clouds. It would take a better man than Perseus to tame the son of Medusa.

Chapter Nine

In-laws

"SPLENDID! SPLENDID!" CRIED King Cepheus over and over again, while Queen Cassiopeia simply wept with joy.

Andromeda sat silent in the circle of Perseus's right arm. She spoke no word of reproach against the parents who had fed her to a sea monster.

Cepheus could not help remembering how he had knelt on the floor and pleaded with Perseus; the boy looked so very young and ragged sitting there, in a borrowed tunic, bloody and bruised and beaming with delight.

"When I woke up this morning, I never thought that this would be my wedding day," said Perseus. "As for the matter of half your kingdom—"

The door burst open then, and Agenor minced into the room on tiptoe, wearing his finest robes and a great many jewels. He ran to Andromeda and would have kissed both her hands if she had not snatched them away. "Dearest darling Andromeda! I am overjoyed at our great good fortune! My prayers have been answered! The gods have spared you!" and he took Andromeda in his arms and kissed her.

Perseus's heart sank a thousand fathoms.

But Andromeda broke away and rapped Agenor sharply across the muzzle as she might a dog that had bitten her. "How dare you! How dare you even speak to me, you coward!"

A dreadful silence fell over the room. Agenor turned very pale, but chose to ignore the trickle of blood leaking from his nose. Turning to the king he said, "When will you make my joy complete, Sire? When shall the wedding be?"

"Ah, well, Count Agenor . . ." began Cepheus haltingly.

He seemed to be in difficulties, so Perseus came to his aid. "Andromeda is going to marry me, sir."

Agenor peered down his nose at Perseus for a moment, then looked round the room with exaggerated astonishment. "Did somebody speak?" he asked.

Andromeda crossed the room and took hold of Perseus's hand. "Perseus of Argos says he is to marry me. It is his reward for saving me and killing the sea monster when there was not a man in Ammon who dared even to speak out for me. I would ask you to stay for the wedding at sunrise, Agenor, but I don't believe dogs are allowed inside the temple of Aphrodite."

Nervously the king whispered something in the queen's ear.

Agenor could not ignore the second insult. He turned on his heel and swept toward the door, head thrown back and the breath whistling in his nostrils. In going, he declared theatrically to everyone present, "Married at sunrise, you say? We shall see about that. We shall see!"

He was no sooner gone from the room than he was forgotten; Agenor had that quality about him. The king might wring his hands and gnaw his lip, but Andromeda and Perseus could think only of their wedding.

The night gardens of Ammon were stripped of flowers to deck the temple of Aphrodite. The statues in the streets were draped with scarfs and streamers so that each time the wind blew, it lent them a kind of dancing life. Andromeda, dressed in a white robe, laid her jewels of gold and lapis lazuli on the altar of the goddess in token of her gratitude for such a husband. And Perseus, in his borrowed tunic and still cluttered with bag and sandals and shield and sword and helmet, clanked his way to the temple on foot rather than alarm people by flying there. He laid aside the weapons at the door of the temple, of course.

Small bells were being rung to welcome bride and groom as the sun hatched out of the land and rose up over the peaceful city of Ammon. And if, offshore, the embittered mermaids hissed and whispered among themselves, their spite could no longer reach the beautiful Princess Andromeda.

Only the spite of Agenor could do that.

As the ceremony began, there came a violent drumming of spear ends against the marble floor, and into the temple, as brash and bullying as drunken schoolboys, came Agenor and twenty, thirty, fifty of his friends and followers.

"Stand aside, boy! A real man has come to fill your place. This is my bride and my wedding. You've kept my place warm for me, but now you can step aside. Agenor is here to arrive a lord and leave a prince."

Perseus looked to the king. It was neither the time nor the place for brawling, and surely the king would send Agenor away with a single word of command? But the king said nothing, and the queen only wept.

Agenor snorted with contempt. "What? Did you think the king would favor you before a count, you thick-necked peacock?"

Andromeda threw back her head in proud disdain. "But I favor him, Agenor. I favor him before you. Who would prize a soldier who hid while the battle was on and claimed the booty when it was over?"

"What does your opinion signify, woman?" piped Agenor. "We are talking kingdoms here, and thrones aren't thrown away on coarse-handed fishermen. Of course he could gut your sea monster! Gutting fish is his trade!" His followers all laughed, loud and long. And suddenly the king had changed sides.

"It's true, Andromeda. Where he comes from they call

87

him One-shirt Perseus. How can you give yourself to a boy they call One-shirt Perseus? How can I share my kingdom with a boy they call—"

The queen joined in, and though Andromeda put her fingers in her ears, she could still hear the soft, insinuating, pleading voice: "Think of it, dear. One-shirt Perseus. It would be a disgrace. We'll give Perseus here money—a lot of money. Then he can go back to catching his fish, and you can marry your childhood sweetheart—your dear Agenor."

Andromeda cried out with revulsion and clung to Perseus, who whispered something into her ear, something not touching on Love.

Meanwhile, the spears had begun to strike the marble floor again. Agenor's followers began to chant over and over again, "One-shirt Perseus! One-shirt Perseus!"

"Stand aside, boy, or we'll cut you down where you stand," said Agenor. Perseus indicated that he had no sword, but Agenor's friends drew out their blades all the same. There were even archers there who laid arrows to their bowstrings and took aim on Perseus's unprotected body. The chanting went on: "One-shirt Perseus! One-shirt Perseus!"

"You didn't stand aside as I told you, boy," said Agenor, wagging his finger. "Now I think it's time for a blood sacrifice on the altar of Aphrodite—to ensure a happy and fruitful marriage between Andromeda and me."

"NO!" Andromeda screamed and covered her eyes.

The archers drew back their bowstrings. The swordsmen were impatient to finish off the work the arrows began.

Impatient. Impatient they stood, and impatient they stand—their weapons up, their teeth bared, their cheeks folded like dogs' masks. They saw Perseus reach inside the pack that lay by his feet. They heard him shout a word or two at Andromeda. They saw the hand draw out something green, repulsive, and writhing. A nasty smell struck their nostrils, and curiosity plucked at their brains. But then their nostrils smelled nothing more, their brains struggled no more after understanding, and their eyes—their eyes that had focused on something so hideous that no eyes should ever have seen it—froze over. Their eyes froze over like winter ice sealing a hundred ponds, and they were stone, stone, stone dead.

The treacherous king and his silly queen sit, even now, like their own statues. The people of Ammon have long since shuffled them away out of sight, ashamed that any king of theirs should break his sworn word. And the Temple of Love is sealed up like a tomb: not a tomb for the frail, loved corpses of the dead, but an everlasting prison for the stony remains of Agenor and his hard-hearted friends.

Perseus returned the head of Medusa to its pack and hoped to lead Andromeda gently out of the temple before she could see what had happened to her mother, father, and one-time suitor. But she opened her eyes and stared round her. She reached out curious fingers to touch the stony arrowheads, the stony eyes, the stony bristles of the fur-trimmed robes.

People say that she was unnatural not to shed a tear, not to rage and run mad, not to shun the man who had turned her mother and father to stone. But after being chained to a rock for a day, waiting for a sea monster to lurch up out of the sea at your feet, who can say how you or I would behave? At any rate, Andromeda turned her back on her mother and father and one-time suitor (whose heart had always been stone anyway). She tied her fate to that of the man they called One-shirt Perseus but who in truth was the son of Zeus.

Chapter Ten

The Reluctant Bride

THERE WAS ANOTHER wedding planned for that self-same day, another royal marriage, another marriage to which the guests came armed with swords.

No sooner had Perseus left on his quest for Medusa's head than King Polydectes made plans for his wedding. All well and good, you might say, since Perseus had gone in search of a wedding present. But Polydectes sent word spurning the little tribal princess named as his future bride. Now that Perseus had gone to certain death, the way was clear for the wedding Polydectes had always intended: to the boy's lovely mother, Danaë.

Danaë woke to find the fisherman Dictys leaning over her.

"Get up, Lady. Quickly. The king's men are coming along the waterfront. I fear the king means to have you, as he always said he would. Get dressed quickly. We must go—leave the country. Polydectes is never going to accept your 'no' for an answer." While Danaë dressed, Dictys grabbed up some flasks of water, some loaves of bread, and a cheese.

"But I can't leave the country, Dictys. How will Perseus ever find us when he comes home?"

The words were in Dictys's mouth to say, "Perseus won't be coming home. By now Perseus is a lump of stone standing in the gritty desert winds, wearing away to a memory." But he could not break Danaë's heart. "Then we shall go to the temple of Athene, Madam, and plead sanctuary. Polydectes won't dare send his troops into a temple; it would bring down the wrath of the gods on his head."

Danaë was pleased by the idea. "And then in a day or two Perseus will be back, and he'll shame the king into abandoning this madness."

Dictys wanted to say, "Perseus won't be home in a day, nor a week, nor a year, nor a lifetime, unless rocks can walk or dead men travel. And the king is too mad with desire to give over his wooing." But what was the purpose in frightening Danaë? So Dictys said nothing, only dragged down a fishing net off the roof rafters and stepped quietly out of doors.

The troops of King Polydectes fell on the little hut as though it were the strongest of fortresses. They attacked with shouts and brandished swords, meaning to cut down the peaceful fisherman and carry away his friend in chains. To their astonishment, Dictys merely looked up from mending a large net spread on a bench before him and did not run for shelter or dash to seize a weapon. Their running faltered; their sword tips dropped.

Then he had them. For he rose up and flung the net. It fell lightly over their heads and entangled every latch of their armor, every thong of their sandals, every finger that tried to throw it off. While the troops lay cursing in the netting, Dictys called Danaë from the hut and ran with her toward the arches, spires, and pillars of the nearby city—to the temple of Athene and to sanctuary among the cold, stony-eyed statues inside it.

Within minutes the temple was surrounded by seven platoons of guards, all brandishing swords, all bellowing for Dictys and Danaë to surrender. The king himself came to stand on the temple steps and shriek his outrage: "I shall have you, Danaë of Argos! I shall have you! How long do you suppose you can hold out against me without food? Without drink? Soon you'll come out of there begging me to marry you. And I shall take you—oh yes, I shall take you, Princess Danaë. But not for a wife. I shall have you for my handmaiden, my slave, my ornament. And do you know the first task you shall do for me? Fasten that fisherman's grinning head on a pole as a warning to anyone else who might be tempted to thwart me. Think on it, Danaë. I, Polydectes, I, King of Seriphus, always have my way in everything. Come out now and beg my forgiveness. On your knees, beg my forgiveness!"

"Wait till Perseus comes! Wait till my son, Perseus, comes home!" cried Danaë's defiant voice from the shadows. "He'll teach you the manners your mother should have taught you!"

"Perseus? One-shirt Perseus? That boy? That braying donkey? He's dead and gone, Lady, dead and gone." And the words splashed through the temple of Athene like icy water, to break upon the altar in a thousand shivering echoes.

After their marriage at a wayside temple, Andromeda and Perseus did not hurry back to Seriphus. They walked and rode and sailed, and now and then Perseus laid aside his luggage and took Andromeda in his arms and flew with her, wearing his winged sandals. But they always had to settle to Earth again by the shining shield, golden sickle sword, the black pack, and battered helmet. Perseus could not bring himself to leave them strewn about on foreign soil like so much litter. As well as helping him complete his task, they made him feel special, fortunate, blessed, smiled on by the gods. "Did I ever tell you how I came to be born?" he said to Andromeda.

"I think you did mention it," she answered patiently. But she did not mind when he told her all over again. She found it very easy to believe that Perseus was the son of Zeus. But then she was in love with him, after all.

The days came and the days went, and the bread and cheese were eaten and the water was gone. Hunger and thirst entered the temple of Athene like stealthy spies in the pay of Polydectes, to drive Danaë and Dictys out into the open.

"Since you saved my life, you have done me kindnesses without number, Dictys," said Princess Danaë after many hours of silence. "Will you do me one last act of friendship?"

"Name it," said the fisherman.

"I would rather die than be a slave to Polydectes. Please, friend. Kill me with that knife of yours and spare me the shame of surrendering."

Dictys, who had been sitting on the steps of the altar carving a piece of wood, dropped his knife in astonishment. "What kind of talk's that? What about Perseus? What about your valiant son? Have you forgotten that he'll be here soon to—"

But Danaë interrupted him. "If I have fooled myself, I'm sure I never fooled you. My reckless, silly Perseus is dead and turned to stone by Medusa. If death could come as quickly to me, I'd welcome it—especially from the hands of a good friend. Will you do this for me, Dictys? Will you kill me before Polydectes loses patience and bursts in here with his soldiers?"

Dictys picked up the knife and studied it for a long time. Then he said, "I'm sorry, Danaë. I can't find it in me to do you that service. The truth is, I've been in love with you for some twenty years now, and it's not in my power to kill someone who's so much a part of me."

Danaë might have wept or she might have laughed, but she only gave one long sigh. "Oh, Dictys, I wish you had said so before now. The truth is, I've loved you myself for quite ten or fifteen years. How very pleasant life could have been." Her voice trailed away as the early morning sounds of the siege army waking and stirring outside ended the silence of the night.

"My patience is gone, Danaë! My siege is over!" King Polydectes' silhouette seemed to fill the bright doorway of the shadowy temple. "Lend me your spear, lieutenant; there's a smell of fish in here. I must harpoon that gaping guppy of a man before I lay hands on my new slave." He came on into the temple, and at his back came a line of soldiers whirling swords so briskly that the air cried out in pain.

From the palisades of heaven, the goddess Athene uttered a scream of outrage—her blood-chilling war cry heard on a thousand battlefields by the dying heroes of the Middle World. "Enter my temple armed, would you, you infidel! Break my sanctuary, would you? Make war on the innocent and soil the white walls of my holiest places with blood?" She drew back her hand, wielding the great spear of war that had not flown since the Siege of Troy. And she took aim on the heart of King Polydectes.

But another hand seized hold of the tail of the spear and wrenched it out of her hand. There stood Hera, queen of heaven. The jealousy burning in her eyes cast strange, green shadows into the hollows of her lovely face and made her curiously grotesque.

Athene protested: "He's defiling my temple! He's breaking my sanctuary!"

"Then you may kill him tomorrow. Today he shall live." Hera's voice was like the keel of a great ship grating on gravel.

"But why, Madam? Why?"

A sneer rifted the features of Zeus's wife and narrowed her large, brown eyes. She spoke in a voice heavy with sarcasm. "Don't tell me that you are the last in heaven to know? That Princess Danaë won the love of my all-glorious husband and bore him a son? Why, the story is all over Olympus! I am the laughingstock of heaven! Listen? Can't you hear them sniggering at me behind their hands? So. This little mortal held Zeus in her arms, did she? Then I have a hankering to see her in the arms of a man less to her liking. Let Polydectes take her. Let him kill the fisherman in front of her very eyes. Then you may throw your spear if you want. But not before. I forbid it."

So Athene laid aside her spear and turned her back on the little creatures of Earth far beneath her. Better not to see, better not to look.

Hera looked. The jealous queen of heaven threw herself down on her stomach, her chin on her hands, and watched the temple in distant Seriphus. The sneer on her face was transformed to a malicious grin. It may have taken her twenty years to find out about Zeus and

Danaë and the tall tower and the shower of gold and the baby boy called Perseus. But now that she knew, somebody must pay. "Bastard," she said under her breath. "Revenge on you, bastard Perseus."

Polydectes put his spear point to Dictys's throat and grinned. "You're a traitor, Dictys, a traitor. You've thwarted the will of your king. You've done your best to stop me from taking what's rightfully mine. I'll sink your boat and I'll burn down your home and I'll bury you at a crossroads where a million feet will trample over your grave!"

Dictys might have replied (though not to plead for his life). But he had the strangest impression that someone was holding him by the scruff of the neck and whispering in his ear: "Close your eyes, Dictys, and whatever happens, don't open them again until I tell you!"

Polydectes reached out a hand and grasped Danaë's arm. "Get up, slave. Get up and kiss me. Then maybe things will go easier for you. Kiss me and tell me you love me."

Danaë might have replied to the king (though not to say that she loved him). But she had the strangest impression that someone was holding her other arm and whispering in her ear: "Close your eyes and whatever happens, don't open them again until I tell you!"

In as long as it takes to lift off a helmet, Perseus appeared on the steps of the altar of Athene. He was carrying no sword, no shield, and wearing no armor, but he carried, across one shoulder, a dark, woven pack. Polydectes thought he must have crept out of the shadows. After the initial surprise, he laughed out loud. "Well! If it isn't One-shirt Perseus come back to defend his mother! Well? Where's my wedding present, you braggart? Where's the head of Medusa you promised me?"

"Here," said Perseus.

"Here." It was the last word Polydectes ever heard spoken. It was the last word ever to lodge in the tiny trembling hairs of his soldiers' ears and tumble into their understanding. "Here."

Then their ears were turned to stone. The temple's burning incense was scentless in their nostrils. The sight of the lovely Danaë and her golden-eyed son blurred and was shut out of their eyes. For they had seen the thing in Perseus's fist—the green, writhing head with its lolling tongue and tusky teeth and staring, staring, glaring Gorgon's eyes.

After he had put away Medusa's head, Perseus had to break the stony fingers of the king to free his mother from the cold, cold grip. He told her and Dictys that they could open their eyes. But Danaë could only look round her for a moment before closing them again in horror.

99

"What have you done, boy?" said Dictys under his breath. "What have you done to all these young men?"

Andromeda came threading her way between the statue-figures of the soldiers and comforted Danaë, who was trembling violently. "It's the looks on their faces!" explained the older woman in a ghastly whisper, and Andromeda said, "I know. I know."

Chapter Eleven

The Games

"FOR THE LOVE of Nature! Take that head away from him before he does any more harm!" Hera, queen of heaven, jabbed her finger into Zeus's giant face. "First Atlas! Then Cepheus and Cassiopeia and now Polydectes and half his royal army! Who next?"

Zeus, too, was furiously angry. He had been found out by his wife, and he hated to be found out.

Hera nagged on and on. "What does he think he's doing? Two royal courts turned to stone! A hundred and fifty people standing about forever and a day, in plain view, in the middle of towns! While Medusa had her den in the middle of a desert, she was only a legend. She didn't kill as many people in a year as Perseus has killed in ten days! He's toting her head about the Central Sea like a traveling magician!"

The laments of a hundred households rose up on the hot midday air and clamored at the gates of heaven, mourning their stony sons and husbands dead at the hands of Perseus. Zeus had been embarrassed by

101

his own son, and he hated above all things to be embarrassed.

Still his wife went on nagging, nagging, nagging him incessantly, carping about the past, harping back to the subject of Danaë. "You don't love me anymore. It's not enough for you that I bring you ambrosia every morning and Hippocrene every night. No! You must go changing yourself into bulls and swans and showers of gold and so forth to win these miserable little mortal women, peopling the world with children too godlike to sit still and too human to handle their magic. Is this all the king of the gods is good for—making mischief among his worshipers? Is it? Well, is it?"

Zeus sprang up suddenly from his throne, and in the shock waves that shook the blue sky, round about a thousand cumulus clouds foundered like galleons. "Silence, woman! Don't you understand anything?" Hera stared in defiance at him until she realized, too late, that he would seize on her and shake her out of heaven's window by her thick, brown hair. "Don't you understand? Fate must take its course! Fate decides everything! We gods have to obey it just as surely as every pig or dog or scorpion down there on Earth! What? Do you suppose I wrote the future in the brains of the oracles? Do you suppose I can change fate to please one jealous, ignorant goddess? At the corner of the world, the Three Fates are spinning the future even now, and nothing I can say—I, the king of the gods!—can change what's destined to happen today or tomorrow or next year or a thousand years from now! It was time for Perseus to be born—that's all. It was time for Medusa to die! The strands of fate had simply come to an end for Cepheus and Cassiopeia and Polydectes! Who will it be today? Do you think you can decide? Do you think you'll be the undoing of my son Perseus, you silly, jealous woman, unless you are the chosen instrument of his fate?" By the time he had finished shaking his wife, a thousand nesting birds had risen up and fled Olympus. (But then that, too, was their fate.) "Now tell Athene to go and get back that death's-head," mumbled Zeus. "Before Perseus can do any more damage. For pity's sake."

But there was no need to wrest the tools of the gods away from Perseus. One glance at his mother's face after the killing of Polydectes, and he immediately laid the bulging black bag on top of the shield on the altar of the goddess of war. To one side he laid the feathered sandals, on the other, the golden sickle sword and Helmet of Invisibility. The stone figures of Polydectes and his troops glared at him as he did so, and by the time he had threaded his way between them to the door and out into the sunlight, he felt like a small boy who has played with fire and accidentally burned down a city. In his bare feet he could no longer fly. He passed a hand through his golden hair and knew he would never again be invisible till his soul drifted free of his body at death.

His hip missed the weight of the sickle sword, and he knew he would kill no more sea monsters.

For a moment he was so overwhelmed by the terrible thought of being ordinary that he dashed back into the temple—pushing through the petrified forest of frozen figures. But when he reached the altar, the sword and sandals were gone, the black bag and helmet had dissolved away, and he was in time only to see the shield reclaimed. It stood on its end, the head of a Gorgon painted in its center—a painting so realistic that Perseus feared for a second that he would be turned to stone by it.

But it was, after all, only a painting, and his flesh remained flesh, and his blood went on running. It ran cold as the goddess herself, Athene, stepped out of the shadows and lifted the shield on her forearm. He would have continued to stare into her gray eyes, for there was something beautiful past bearing in them. But she lifted her shield until its topmost rim covered her face and only the feathered crest of a warrior's helmet showed above the shimmering metal. He was forced to close his eyes against the blinding brightness.

And when he opened them again, Athene had gone. She left her temple astride the winged horse Pegasus, which she rode back to the slopes of Olympus. Those who glimpsed her flight through the sky said they had seen a new goddess in the heavens bearing a shield too fearful to describe and mounted on a winged horse.

Nothing remained for Perseus. Nothing? The beauty

and love of Andromeda? The kingdom of Seriphus? The treasures of Ammon? Perhaps, after all, he was a little better off than before he left on his quest, when his only possession was the nickname One-shirt Perseus.

"You must choose your throne, Perseus," said Dictys. "You can't go about casting down kingdoms and leaving whole nations without a leader. The time for adventuring is over. Maybe you won't prove a better king than Polydectes or Cepheus, but you must at least try. Andromeda will help you. Well? Where will you make your kingdom?"

Perseus was horrified. He was not yet twenty years old. Except for a few overcrowded weeks, he had done nothing, been nowhere, met no one, learned nothing except about catching fish and killing monsters. It was no apprenticeship for wearing a crown.

At last he said to Dictys and Danaë, "This is my wish. You two shall rule over Seriphus on my behalf—on the condition that you marry and move to the palace. It doesn't seem right for a king and queen to live in a fisherman's hut. Then, if you'll give me your fishing boat, Andromeda and I will sail to Argos, the land where I was born. I shall make my peace with my grandfather and tell him everything that's happened to us. I tell you, Mother, I can't rest easy until I know just why he locked you in that tower or why he set us both on the sea to drown."

"I don't bear him any grudge," said Danaë, taking Dictys's big, gnarled hands in her own. "Everything has turned out for the best. I hope you don't harbor any thoughts of revenge."

Perseus's face was a picture of innocence. "Why would I bear a grudge, Mother? Look what fate has brought me." And he took hold of Andromeda's small, soft, white hand. "But I don't want to be a king just yet, so let me make this one last journey. Please."

There was no more hope of dissuading him than of dissuading a river from giving itself to the sea. He set sail before the week was out, with Andromeda to help him raise the sail and cook the sardines he caught on a line dangled into the wake of the little boat.

"He is coming, Acrisius! He is coming!"

The tower in the courtyard came striding on tree-root legs and bent its shoulders and pushed a human face up against the window of King Acrisius's chamber. The cell bars took the shape of a toothy mouth, which writhed and grinned as it whispered, "Here comes your fate, as the oracle promised! Here comes your grandson to smash in your head!"

Acrisius gave a scream and awoke standing by the window with his arms pushed out into the night to fend off his nightmare. One step more and he might have plunged to his death in the courtyard below.

He mopped his brow on the curtain and called feebly for his page to help him back to bed. "Tell the admiral to make ready the fastest ship in the fleet. I've got to . . . I've got to . . . leave Argos for a while. Never mind why. If my ministers of state ask you where I've gone, tell them I've . . . no, no. Better nobody knows. Don't tell anybody. But alert all the ports along the coast and tell them to keep a sharp lookout for any ship carrying a traitor called Perseus. An assassin called Perseus. You hear? A thousand pieces of gold to anyone who kills Perseus before he can set foot in Argos. He's coming. I'm sure of it. The same dream every night for a week. He's coming! And I won't stay here to be murdered in my own bed! Put the army on full alert!"

The sleepy page only half listened to the old king's ranting. The army of Argos had been on full alert for a year, and the ports kept watch night and day for the "traitor" Perseus, who had driven the king half mad merely by staying alive.

Rumors had traveled as far as Argos of superhuman deeds of courage performed by a youth with golden eyes called Perseus—a boy loved by the gods, armed with magic and terrible in the destruction of his enemies. So eager was King Acrisius for news that he paid sea captains whole chests of gold to hear stories of Perseus's exploits. Then when he heard their news, he had them thrown headfirst into the harbor for daring to say that Perseus was still alive.

When he fled Argos in terror, for two days he would not tell the captain of the ship which way to steer. He would not name a destination because he could not think himself where to go. All he wanted was to run to some corner of the Earth where Perseus would not find him. Let the boy seize his throne. Let the boy claim Argos for his own. Just as long as Acrisius did not have to die. Just as long as the oracle's prediction was wrong. Just as long as Acrisius could go on living, could go on living. . . .

You might ask yourself what kind of a life it was to cling to—racked with nightmares and haunted by guilty fear. But to some men death is so infinitely terrifying that they spend their whole lives running away from it, as though it were a dog on their heels. They never have breath or time enough to enjoy living.

"Truly, Sire, I cannot help but ask you again—which way must I steer?" said the ship's captain as patiently as he knew how. "I must put in for ship's stores if nothing else." The king looked at him—suspicious, terrified. "If I might suggest it, Your Majesty, why not call in at Larissa in Thessaly? See the Games. Watch the athletes. They say there's no finer entertainment on all the shores of the Central Sea—javelin, discus, high jump, footraces, wrestling. . . ."

"Yes, yes. All right," snapped the king. "But listen here! When we dock in Thessaly, no word of where you're from or who I am. Right? I don't have a name. Anonymous. Nobody. Understood?"

"Nobody," repeated the captain obediently. And it seemed to him, looking at the little hunched creature muffled up in its cloak, darting fearful glances over his shoulder at every squeal of the gulls, that King Acrisius was right. He was nobody. Nobody at all.

The Games at Larissa were a riot of fanfares and flags, processions and presentations. Young men in white tunics, wearing their muscles like snake wrestlers, stood about the arena, dusty to the knees and bleached gold by the sun. The tiered seats of the amphitheater banked up toward the bright blue sky in multicolored rings, and acrobats were performing sideshows for the queues of people still hopeful of buying seats.

Perseus and Andromeda, who had interrupted their voyage to Argos to watch the Games, were standing near the entrance drinking cooled wine when the prince of Thessaly himself stopped for refreshment. He eyed the Princess Andromeda from head to foot and decided he was in the company of nobility.

"And whom have I the pleasure of addressing?" he inquired, flourishing the hem of his short cloak as he bowed.

"Perseus of Ammon, Seriphus, and Argos," said Perseus, recollecting how he had once been called One-shirt Perseus.

The prince was quite put off his stride. He broke off his elaborate bow and popped upright. "Zeus! Really? What, the hero who cut off Medusa's head and killed Poseidon's sea monster? Zeus! Really? Why wasn't I told?" Perseus blushed. A little crowd began to gather. "But why aren't you competing? The whole idea of the Games is that the best from all nations should compete with each other! What's your sport? Running? Jumping? No! Javelin, of course!"

"Well, actually I . . ." Perseus, who had grown up working, without ever a moment for sport, racked his brains to think what sport he might have been good at if he had had the time. As Dictys's apprentice, it had been his task to throw out the marker buoy at the tail of each fishing net. He said, "Discus. That's my sport. Throwing the discus." And before he knew it, the prince of Thessaly had hurried him away to the competition tents to chalk his hands and choose a discus from the rack of shining pottery discuses. They looked for all the world like a row of kitchen plates.

Perseus was flattered. He was confident. He watched the other discus throwers whirling themselves round on one foot before hurling the discus off the palm of one hand and out across the arena, and he was certain he could throw his just as far. Had he not the strength of a god in his shoulder blades, the power of an Immortal in his blood?

"Good luck," said Andromeda and kissed him before hurrying away to find a seat among the crowd.

"And now! As a guest of the prince of Thessaly himself, a late entrant in the discus throwing!" bellowed the crier, his words whirling up the great dished sides of the arena. "Perseus of Ammon, Seriphus, and Argos!"

Perseus rubbed more chalk into his palms because they were sweating.

Acrisius, sitting behind the throwing circle, in the third tier of seats, felt sweat pour down his brow and back and hands. He shuddered violently, so that the girl newly sat down beside him asked if he was ill. "No!" he said. "No," and peered through spread fingers toward the throwing circle and the young man standing there.

His hair was an upward rush of gold, like a volcanic eruption; his arms and legs were scarred and bruised from some recent fight; his eyes were golden slits closed down against the sunshine, like the coins posted into the mouth of a dead man. . . . He was beautiful. He reminded Acrisius very much indeed of his daughter, Danaë, the daughter he had loved so much.

Perseus spun himself round, shoulders down, arms outstretched. The crowd laughed at his appalling style— but they had to cheer the great long throw he made—a man's length farther than any other discus on the field. The stadium fell silent as Perseus made ready for his second throw.

Watching, anonymous, just one man hidden among the thousands of other spectators, knowing he would not be recognized even if the boy saw him, Acrisius was struck by a sudden torrent of happy thoughts. This is my grandson. This is my heir. This perfect, beautiful young man bears my family name. This is what that helpless little baby grew into—a man who can throw a discus farther than any man else; a man who can slay sea

111

monsters and cut off a Gorgon's head; a man famed throughout the Middle World; a man with the blood of gods flowing through his veins; a man already a legend, already a myth; a man, if ever there was one, to strike pride into his grandfather's heart.

He could not help it. He could not stop himself. Acrisius reached out his old, veined hand and plucked the robe alongside him. "That's my grandson out there," he whispered, and his eyes were full of tears so that he did not clearly see what happened next.

Perseus mistimed his second throw. He let go of the discus a half turn too soon, and instead of it flying out across the arena, across the measuring marks on the ground, it curled out of the back of the throwing circle and into the crowd.

There was silence, then a rising clamor of curiosity. "Where did it fall? Was anybody hit? Is anybody hurt?"

Andromeda looked down at the old man lying in her lap. The discus had struck him in the head, but it was a clean blow and there was no blood. He looked simply as if he were asleep, and a single tear had crept out of one eye and down his cheek.

"He said he was your grandfather," was all she could tell Perseus when he came climbing up the tiers of seats like a madman, tearing at his golden hair and rending at his clothing with chalky hands. Choking with remorse, he lifted up the old man's body and carried it out of the stadium, weeping aloud.

Chapter Twelve

Blind Fate

"IT WAS FATE, not you, that killed Acrisius." That's what they all said. "It was foretold by the oracle. It was written in the stars before you were born. It was Acrisius's fate to die like that!"

But Perseus would not be comforted. He crouched over the body of his grandfather and wept for three days and nights. Then he placed it on the foredeck of his boat and continued on his journey to Argos—a coming home for the dead king and a coming home, too, for Perseus after nearly twenty years of exile.

News traveled ahead of the little boat, and by the time it put into port, the streets of Argos were lined with crowds. The statues were draped with scarfs and the ground strewn with flowers. Flags beckoned him into port, and a mob waited to greet him.

"Hail to Perseus, slayer of Medusa, slayer of Poseidon's sea monster, and heir to the throne of Argos! Hail to him who killed the mad tyrant Acrisius and closed his mouth forever! Hail to Perseus, King of Argos!"

Perseus leaped over the prow of the boat and scattered the mob with his fists and with curses. "Silence! Hold your tongues! Death to the next man who calls me King of Argos! There's the King of Argos—on my foredeck! Give him the funeral of a king and drape the houses in black—not like this with flowers and ribbons! What kind of men are you to rejoice at an old man's death?"

"But he was a tyrant!" said the women of Argos, open-mouthed. "Just like Cepheus and Polydectes, and you turned them into stone! You're a hero, so you are. Everybody says so." And they stared after him as he climbed the harbor path, and wondered.

For three days more Perseus locked himself away in the palace and sat at the window of Acrisius's bedchamber and stared out at the spot where the long-demolished tower had once stood: his birthplace. At last Andromeda came to him and said, "Think what Dictys told you. It's time to be a king. Don't think badly of yourself. You're a hero, after all. Everybody says so."

Then he covered his face with his hands and rocked to and fro on the window seat. "No, Andromeda. Don't you see? If it was fate for me to kill Acrisius—and the gods know I didn't mean to!—then it was fate for me to kill the sea monster, fate for you to love me, fate for Medusa to fall to my sword. I didn't do anything! It doesn't matter what I do; everything will turn out just the same. The Fates are weaving the future now. They have been since the start of Time and they'll go on until there is no more thread and Time itself comes to an end. I'm nothing. I'm no one. I'm a puppet dangling on that cord the Fates are weaving. There's no such thing as a hero—only a man with a destiny. Not the great traveler Odysseus, not Theseus the Minotaur-slayer, not even the giant Hercules. And not me, for all my bragging. Everything we ever did— good or bad—was no more than our role in an everlasting play. Tomorrow I'll go to see the oracle at Epidaurus and ask what lies in store for me. Then I'll know everything that's planned. What else is there to know?"

The ministers of state had shyly gathered outside the door. They pleaded with him, stretching out before them the crown of Argos on a golden tray: "Lord Perseus, be our king! Give us a king! We must have a king!" But he slammed the doors on them.

"Never! Never! I'll never wear that crown! There's blood on it. Blood!" The ministers went sadly away, thinking that Acrisius's grandson was proving just as mad as Acrisius had been.

They did not argue when he exchanged realms with King Megapenthes, who ruled over an insignificant little kingdom along the coast from Argos—a land of shepherds and fishermen and vineyards and olive trees.

On his way to the temple at Epidaurus, Perseus was surprised not to pass any travelers coming away from the shrine. And when he arrived, the place seemed deserted. The door of the dank, dark sanctuary was strung with cobwebs, and no tributes lay on the steps, only a plate holding a little dirty rainwater.

He ducked inside and could see nothing. The torches along the walls were burned down to extinguished stumps, and the dish of holy oil had long since burned away on the marble altar. In the thick, touchable darkness Perseus stumbled up against the tarnished rods of the tripod itself—the throne of the serpent oracle. Something hissed close by his ear. For a moment his blood ran cold as he recalled the snake-haired Medusa.

"What do you want? Who are you? Get out and leave me in peace-ce-ce."

"Is that the oracle? Are you here? I can't see you. I'm Perseus of . . . I'm Perseus, son of Danaë, come to learn what the future holds for me."

Something smooth-scaled touched his body and reared up; the pale diamond of a snake's head lunged toward his face. "Don't you know? Haven't you heard? Why mus-s-t you torment me like this-s-s? I'm blind. I'm us-seless-s to you, Pers-seus-s-s. I'm blind, blind, blind!" The snake interrupted itself. "Pers-seus-s? I remember that name. You were to kill your grandfather, Acris-sius-s-s of Argos-s. Is-s he dead yet?"

Perseus said nothing, choking on tears.

"Nobody comes-s to tell me, you know? No one comes-s to tell me how the world runs-s. For centuries-s I told them the future. Now I'm not us-seful to them, and they leave me in ignorance. And no one pays-s tribute!"

"You're blind?" said Perseus slow-wittedly. "How? Blind?"

"S-someone has cut the threads-s of Fate. With shears, so they say. Sh-shears! Ah! They might as well have sh-sheared through the stalks of my very eyes-s. My inward s-sight is gone. I who looked into the future can s-see nothing. Nothing! As blind as the Cyclops after Odyss-seus-s drove in his sharpened stick. Blind! Now nothing is certain. Nothing is s-s-sure. The s-strands-s-s of fate are cut! The future is cut loos-se like a sh-ship that cuts-s-s anchor!"

Perseus felt about for the snake's weaving head and held its scaly hood between his two hands. "The gods of Olympus bless you with everlasting darkness! You've told me the best news a man could ever hear!"

The serpent pulled away from him, unaccustomed to the touch of human hands. "But now I sh-shall s-s-starve for want of tributes-s-s, s-starve for want of worshipers-s!"

"You shall never starve," promised Perseus. "I, King Perseus of Little Tiryns, swear it. I will shower you with tributes! I swear it! Don't you understand? At last every man and god is free of those spinners in the corner of the world. They had us trapped like flies in a spider's web, the Three Fates. But now we're free to be cowards or heroes or madmen or kings or fishermen or fathers or fools! Our futures are our own to make!"

And he ran with the serpent in his arms, outside the cave, where, for the first time in centuries, it blinked its

117

lidless eyes at the sights of the present world. It trembled in his arms, afraid of the light.

The oracle could no longer see into the future. For the future lay unwoven, invisible . . .

. . . like a child in the womb waiting to be born . . .

. . . like a bottomless well of untasted water . . .

. . . like a page of white paper still to be written upon by Perseus and the heroes who came after him.